AF424283

MARFA LIGHTS

STEVEN MARKOFF

SEVEN GABLES
PRESS

ISBN (paperback): 979-8-218-41791-8
ISBN (hardcover): 979-8-218-41792-5
Library of Congress Control Number: 2024907231

This is a work of fiction. Any references to real people, events, establishments, products, services, or locales are intended only to manufacture a sense of reality and authenticity and are used fictionally. All other names, characters, and places, and all dialogue and incidents portrayed in this novel are the product of the author's imagination.

Edited by Leah LoScudo Stern
Cover by Jarob Bramlett of Quiet Strength Design
Special thanks to Naomi Spier and Cari Montgomery

Published by Seven Gables Press
1st Edition 2024

10 9 8 7 6 5 4 3 2 1

For my parents,
If you would've pushed me harder, I could've been Derek Jeter.
But you still did a terrific job.

Dear Marfa,
Despite the cynicism of this book,
you've remained my great escape for nearly two decades.
Thank you!

The truth is rarely pure and never simple.
– Oscar Wilde, *The Importance of Being Earnest*

The eyes are the windows to your soul.
– William Shakespeare

MARFA LIGHTS

I'm having the dream again. Or should I say the nightmare? It always starts off pleasantly enough. A vision of my gorgeous mother, face glowing in the moonlight. Complexion paralleling women ten years her junior: no knives, no needles, no nothing. Contrary to the majority of females, she welcomed aging. Well, didn't shy from it anyway. Her beauty, however, proved more than skin-deep. She fostered her elderly parents during the latter stages, refusing to let them ride out their days at a nursing home. Giving back became her passion, donating both time and money assisting those less fortunate. Yet the most selfless act – supporting her true love and raising the newborn they conceived together.

Then there's my handsome father: salt-and-pepper hair, strong bone structure, cleft chin. A debonair older gentleman in peak physical condition, chalked up to a training regimen instilled amid the high school football era, which carried across his military service and sustained eternal. Beyond the outward appearance shone the sweetest human you'd ever encounter. That rare soul who could put people at ease and make them feel as if they were the center of the universe. He maintained but two reasons for living – his wife and son. To him, family wasn't everything… it was the only thing.

This perfect couple is currently stationed in a moving vehicle. Mom hears Dad causing a ruckus behind her. The customarily vivacious constitution sours while her spouse's own frustration level swells. Whatever he's straining to accomplish isn't working, and the epitome of serenity grows enraged. Words are swapped, and a squabble ensues. She rotates her body, aiming to defuse the aforementioned dilemma. As a result, the calm dissipates, and his temper loses way. The struggle escalates rapidly – neither willing to concede. He clasps her limbs, striving to force a return, and they tussle.

Suddenly, something strikes the automobile. The scene downshifts into slow motion. Shattered glass floats through the air, and my folks take flight. Fraught with panic and despair, they lock onto each other. A lifetime's worth of cherished memories oscillating between them in a frenetic split-second. Before that last breath, their gaze swivels, and the fear subsides. A glimpse of the boy they so proudly reared yields a smile, even as survival hangs in the balance.

With imminence on the horizon, the jovial countenance diminishes. Their lips part, eliciting one final plea. The declaration reverberates like shouts inside a canyon. Though crystal clear, the meaning is unintelligible. I vocalize the statement, laboring to decipher the context. At the precise instant they're being vacuumed into the abyss, my hand instinctively extends toward them. It's a vain attempt at salvation. The outstretched organ gradually retracts, and darkness fills the frame. But that nonsensical phrase lingers, repeating itself over and over and over – "*Open your eyes.*"

THE MOST WONDERFUL TIME OF THE YEAR

I fucking hate Christmas. And not due to any of the hundreds of pedestrian rationales you might expect. I'm totally cool with candy canes, Jimmy Stewart, a white elephant, The Grinch, door-to-door carolers, Ralphie Parker, the smell of Frasier Fir, and Rudolph. As far as the pickle ornament, Bing Crosby, non-consensual mistletoe, Frosty the Snowman, overcrowded shopping malls, Mariah Carey, moronic inflatable decorations, and Charles Dickens are concerned, it's Kumbaya, my Lord. Stockings on the mantle, Judy Garland, obnoxious blinding lights, The Muppets, imbecilic photo collage cards, Clark Griswold, ugly sweaters, and even that obese, bearded chimney sweep donning the red velvet costume provoke zero issues whatsoever.

Nah, the stimulus instigating the hatred is appreciably graver. It's the date my parents were killed in a car accident. The details escape me because, according to multiple specialists and numerous psychiatrists, I've successfully blocked the entire incident from my mind. I was diagnosed with a litany of traumas comprising varying degrees of amnesia and am unable to retain a shred of evidence regarding the case. There's an appellation for it. Lamentably, I don't remember that either.

Since I'm incapable of ascertaining the exact nature of the tragedy, I've concocted a credible tale to respond to inquiries. It involves a trip out west on Jesus' birthday. Mom and dad driving their Lexus along a two-lane highway and colliding with an oncoming sedan. All parties died on impact, and guilt wasn't established. Some of the intricacies change, now and then, but the gist stays the same.

Oftentimes, I'm left wondering if what I suspect occurred is purely in my subconscious. I recall the original analyst tasked me with keeping a journal. His instructions specified to tote it around constantly, jotting down anything that popped into my head, relating to their deaths. The caveat – avoid reading the previous entries; sheerly chronicle my thoughts and forge ahead.

Six weeks into our sessions, he requested I bring the notebook to deconstruct. As he delivered the first entry aloud, an undeniable sensation of relief washed over me. Had I experienced a breakthrough? Did this baloney actually succeed? It appeared I'd participate in a non-fictional *Good Will Hunting* moment. A narrative whereupon I, Matt Damon, embrace him, Robin Williams, then weep in light of my recovery. But the minute he flipped the page and recited the follow-up passage, I snapped back to reality. It was completely different. Then he reeled off the next annotation and the one after that, and so on and so forth, until I abandoned belief.

My psyche paradoxically conjured a myriad of plausible stories, scenarios, and outcomes surrounding the episode. Ultimately, I arrived at the conclusion that no matter how long I tried or whichever technique I undertook, grasping the circumstances would demonstrate insurmountable – at least consistently. So, why bother? I had exhausted infinite intervals seeking the truth, yet my brain rejected preserving the data.

For the sake of argument, suppose I awakened someday, and the facts turned transparent. They'd still be deceased, and I'd still be Oliver Twist. Alternately, I made peace with the notion they lived their lives to the fullest. That each symbolized the dictionary definition of a "good person." And most importantly, that they cared about me so goddamn much they wouldn't want me subsisting in a perpetual depressive state, reflecting on the past. Instead, demanding I move forward and never look back.

Although it may sound morbid, all things considered, every winter I honor their passing by embarking on a cross-country expedition. Early November is traditionally when I tackle the "where" portion. I log ideas as they present themselves, but it's usually a month prior that I pinpoint the location. Upon reaching a verdict, I confide in a few trusted allies in the event of an emergency.

It's the sole opportunity I'm afforded to get off-the-grid, hence my whereabouts remaining classified. This go-round won't deviate from the plan except, for once, I've selected the destination beforehand. Ladies and germs, drumroll please… Without further ado, I'm happy to announce come this Friday, December 18th, I'll take my talents to the small West Texas town of Marfa, population 1788.

LOVE IS A BATTLEFIELD

It's Tuesday at 2:45 p.m., and I'm hustling to my biweekly 3:00 p.m. therapy appointment. When I initiated the psychiatry, Dr. What's His Nuts advocated incorporating a therapist. They regularly operate conjointly to dispatch a quote, unquote, 'comprehensive mental health treatment.' How it was articulated gave every indication of aiding the process. Sigmund Fraud renders his judgment on the specific disorder he claims I'm plagued with, subsequently prescribing the integral medications to manage it. The therapist and I then talk through the problem to obtain a clearer understanding, simultaneously combating the sentiments enveloping the affliction, yada yada yada.

Initially, I hesitated. It seemed I'd be coerced into regurgitating the identical exchanges concerning my folks twice. Moreover, as an only child bereft of any biological relatives, I had nowhere else to turn for advice. In consequence, I acquiesced to the double team. Figured I owed it to Mom and Dad to give it the old college try, praying something panned out… *Epic fail.* The worst part – the pharmaceuticals made me lethargic, which sucked for a degenerate who conventionally relished ingesting drugs.

While I wound up not lending credence to the psychiatric attribute of the spectrum, there were definite merits to the therapeutic angle. I philosophized that these counselors are essentially life coaches, furnishing guidance via discussion. Their goal isn't to fix you per se; it's to listen with the intention of gaining insight, then tender suggestions to facilitate smarter decision making. That's what appealed to me. Therefore, I summoned the courage to sack the physicians, and it felt like a huge weight lifted off my shoulders. Thankfully, I persevered with the therapy.

My shrink's name is Julie. In total disclosure, I chose her based upon looks. I ain't sayin' she's hot; I'm just sayin' she's a cut above the rest. Once I resolved to take a crack at this, I phoned my insurance provider. The customer service rep told me to hop online and choose from a directory of caregivers in my network. Googling each candidate and hinging my selection on facial features couldn't have been the tactic they prognosticated I'd deploy, but I'm a renegade… or a slimeball.

See, the ex-psychiatrists nominated the former therapists. Predictably, we didn't synergize. I determined that for this to produce the desired effect, wiping the slate clean was pivotal. The situation required a professional unapprised of my familial history and could view me as an individual, rather than a case study. Plus, tolerating my charming, yet moderately offhanded charisma would prove mandatory.

During our inaugural tête-à-tête, she outlined her two basic rules. Rule number one – if I was suicidal or a threat to myself or others, she'd recommend an involuntary hold for evaluation. Rule number two – if I was abusive toward kids, she'd notify the proper authorities straightaway. I assured her my devout narcissism wouldn't sanction suicide and that I hadn't sired rug rats – none I knew of anyhow.

Shortly thereafter, she asked where I wanted to begin. Back then, my cardinal quandaries encompassed a perverse, juvenile BMX bicycle infatuation and a crush on a diminutive nineteen-year-old boasting a yummy, apple-shaped derrière. Ventilating my O.G. Hutch Trick Star that paraded an ACS rotor and rims, Aerospeed cranks, bear trap pedals, Woody Itson handlebars, and a Kashimax saddle wasn't the first impression I aspired to provision; ergo, I deemed the Lolita a suitable launching pad.

On account of my incurable ailment, clinically labeled 'foot-in-mouth syndrome,' I broke the ice by asserting, "I'm sleeping with this little girl." Julie, gaping in awe, stopped the session immediately. I cringed remorsefully, clarified the proclamation, and she accepted my apology.

For the record, she couldn't resist snickering, realizing I was gonna be a handful. Nearly a decade has elapsed, and I daresay that's roughly the length I've stripped off her lifespan.

The hour primarily resembles a stand-up comedy routine as I channel my inner-Chappelle and relay outrageous anecdotes from my decadent, overprivileged upbringing. Periodically, I'll end by quipping, "That's all the time we have." It supplies her profuse satisfaction. Nevertheless, when the shit hits the fan, our talks help enormously.

Whereas I've hinted I'm apprehensive to discuss my parents, we've obviously broached the subject. Despite respecting that I preferred not to dwell on it or focalize it, Julie contended intermittent examinations were beneficial. Thus, I'll assent to her slipping tidbits into the discourse contingent upon centralizing themes of paramount importance, otherwise known as the shallow facets of my day-to-day world.

I park and jog toward the office. Penetrating the lobby, I notice her door slightly ajar. I should knock. It's impolite to intrude. What if she's...? Oops-a-daisy, too late.

Julie's nestled in her chair, nape contorting, supremely familiar with my shtick. "And how are we this afternoon?" she investigates, twirling to herald me.

"We are fabulous," I stress, sprawled atop the green velour chaise. "Just three days 'til Christmas vacation!"

"Ah yes, your beloved Christmas."

"Damn skippy. I'm feeling extra festive this holiday season."

"Delightful."

"Before we delve into my staggering array of emotional and mental conundrums, there's a question I've been dying to ask you."

"I'm all ears."

"Why does Western civilization neglect to acknowledge Santa is an anagram for Satan?"

"Um... On that note, let's resume where we left off."

"Et tu, Brute? Fine." I unite my palms and rub them vigorously, reminiscent of Mr. Miyagi mending Danielson's fractured leg. "Let the healing commence."

"Previously, we addressed the characteristics behind your ideal woman. You insisted I permit you a chance to deliberate. Have you done that?"

"Absolutely. Underwent an extensive introspection. Ready?"

"Spill it."

"Sparkling personality, fantastic sense of humor, receptive to procreation, values food and alcohol, athletic but doesn't live in the gym, and competent enough to maintain a conversation. Those represent the principal elements. Oh, and boobs. Great boobs."

"Of course. Spectacular breasts are vital in connection to finding your soulmate," she affirms cynically.

"Glad you agree."

"Any recent developments?"

"Got a date tonight."

"That's exciting."

"Meh, I don't anticipate it leading anywhere."

"Expound."

"Well, she's extremely attractive. Unfortunately, our text banter is pretty mundane, and her Instagram posts are exclusively selfies. On the surface, not the sharpest tool in the shed."

"Then why go to the trouble?"

"Didn't you hear me? She's extremely attractive," I parrot smugly.

"Okay, forget the alluring bimbo."

"Wow, that's harsh, Julie. She might harbor a cornucopia of exceptional qualities."

"Uh-huh. How's the quest for Mrs. Right progressing?"

"Horrible. Zoe Saldana's married, Zooey Deschanel and Zoey Deutch are spoken for, and Zoë Kravitz... unattainable."

"Can we take this seriously?"

"I'm sorry. I mask pain with tomfoolery. As you were."

"Where've you been searching?"

"Hmm?"

"Are you utilizing dating apps or websites?"

"Hell no."

"Then through which medium do you foresee interacting with eligible women?"

"Beats me. Probably the reason I'm single, I guess. Assumed I'd be hitched by now."

"Perhaps it's time to modernize. I met my hubby on eHarmony."

"Ew, gross."

"I'll inform him you said that."

"Jeez Louise, don't get your panties in a wad. I'm sure he's terrific, but I cannot put stock in that stuff. Anyone professing to download Bumble, Tinder, Grindr, etcetera for purposes beyond hooking up is lying or stupid. Regardless, that isn't my objective. There's an abundance of babes I could conduct a strictly lascivious relationship with, and that's not to say I'm anything special. I recognize exactly what I am."

"And what's that?"

"A cumulative eight point five."

"Really?"

"Nine on a good day. Mix liquor into the equation, and I'm Harry Styles."

With eyebrows hoisted, she chuckles, thoroughly entertained. "Continue."

"I was merely venting the whole sexual component becomes tiresome. Nobody trusts me when I reveal I'm craving significantly more. Even my nearest and dearest speculate I'm full of crap for proposing I wanna settle down. Whether it's my occupation, my schedule, or my overall attitude, I'm never perceived as the guy pursuing intimacy and stability.

"To add insult to injury, I'm tight with an older crew, tenacious in their endeavors to convince me marriage personifies pure evil. A large percentage of them can't stand their wives. Some of them can't stand their children. I'm dangerously close to throwing in the towel and testing monkhood. The odds aren't in my favor here, and I'm no spring chicken."

"No, you certainly are not," she concurs snarkily.

"Oho, look at the therapist getting cute."

"Kidding aside, I'll swallow your concession that you're suffering complications procuring the cited prerequisites. Conversely, I'm hearing an aversion to integrate the resources at your disposal. You've declined the digital approach yet spend the brunt of your leisure time fraternizing with a group who, by your own admission, don't contribute toward meeting potential love interests. And your daily ritual doesn't loan itself to branching out either. You're running on the proverbial hamster wheel as it pertains to the manner in which you're introduced to members of the opposite gender. So… What do you intend to do about it?"

I ruminate over the probe. Julie's voice conveys an earnestness, and I opt to reply humbler than normal. "Honestly, I'm stumped. As cocky as I am in particular aspects, I'm equally as afraid in others. I've always possessed this underlying thirst to control everything, and this is the key area that's lacking. Theoretically, why I turn tail whenever prospects arise. I've gone out with impressive chicks, yet invariably uncover flaws in them."

"Elucidate."

"There was one that checked all the boxes, but she had misshapen nostrils."

"Misshapen nostrils?"

"Her nose holes weren't symmetrical, and I became obsessed. Another gal wore extensions and didn't warn me."

"Big whoop. Lots of ladies sport them. It's quite common."

"Be that as it may, when I leaned in for a kiss and clutched the back of her hair, I fondled the clip, got spooked, and accidentally tore a piece off."

Julie crows at the absurdity. "What else?"

"Went to dinner with a dame who started every sentence using the word 'literally.' I blew a gasket and ditched her at the restaurant. A separate female used 'supposably' in lieu of supposedly and misapplied it, just the same. 'Do you enjoy sushi? Supposably.' Romanced a stunning librarian. Sadly, she was a major-league Catholic."

"And…?"

"Exit only, and I won't ride the Hershey Highway," I euphemize, winking. Julie isn't amused. I'm cognizant of this ascribable to inheriting her death stare reserved for junctures I agitate her immensely. "My bad, I crossed the line."

"Wrap it up," she dictates.

"It's possible I'm a superficial asshole un…"

"Shocking."

"Let me finish."

"By all means."

"It's possible I'm a superficial asshole unwilling to take the plunge, so I formulate excuses to sabotage myself. The thing is, I'm not lonely. I preserve an active social life, and work keeps me sufficiently busy. In spite of that, having a girlfriend sounds nice. Somebody I can brunch with on Sundays. A partner I could lie beside and watch a flick. Someone who'll inspire me to… be better. I simply don't command the fortitude nor ambition to woo a gaggle of randos, crossing my fingers I hit the jackpot. I'm a creature of habit, and yeah, maybe my methods are antiquated, but it shouldn't warrant venturing outside my comfort zone."

"But if you're reluctant to broaden your horizons, then how will these pitfalls alter henceforth?"

I shrug glumly. "They won't, and I've reconciled being alone."

"You're telling me you're prepared to brave bachelorhood until your dream girl magically blossoms out of thin air?"

"What choice is there? Evidently, I haven't exerted the compulsory effort, and the pittance I've exercised hasn't been rewarding. And that's why I'm destined for eccentric cat lady reclusion unless you play matchmaker."

"Oh, it's at the top of my docket," she jeers flippantly. "I am of the opinion, albeit presumably in the vast minority, that you've got a lot to offer, and I'm genuinely rooting for ya."

"HA! Awfully kind. Don't worry, just going through a rough patch. And your boy's well-versed in weathering the storm of disappointment. I was born a Cleveland Browns supporter."

"Whaddaya say we switch gears?"

"Yabba Dabba Doo."

"The fabled Marfa."

"Now we're talking. Bring it on, Kirsten."

"We've canvassed this topic ad nauseam. No last-minute reversal?"

"Naw, it's already planned and paid for."

"What if the journey doesn't fulfill expectations?"

"I'm staying optimistic even though the probability for letdown is astronomical, especially with the magnitude I've overhyped this place. But if it blows, I'll bail. Nothing provides me greater pleasure than the purity and isolation of the road, so I'm peachy hopping back inside the car and plowing ahead. Could get my kicks on Route 66 or honky-tonk in Nashville or Mardi Gras my tuchus off along Bourbon Street. The sky's the limit, sister."

"I have the utmost confidence it'll be amazing. Wish I were able to tour the town in the flesh."

"I'll snap plenty of pictures to show you."

"Speaking of pictures, I'd hoped you'd partake in an extracurricular activity."

"You're assigning me homework?"

"I wouldn't necessarily categorize it as homework. Do you own a Polaroid?"

"The camera that ejects the photo, then you shake it? What year is this? You've heard of the iPhone, correct?"

"Firstly, they advise against shaking the negative. By doing so, causes damage to the image and…"

"Whoa, whoa, whoa, whoa," I interrupt reproachfully. "You callin' André 3000 a liar?"

"Indeed, I am."

I gasp. "Blasphemy!"

She grins and nudges, "Can you get your hands on one or not?"

"Uh, ten seconds ago, I was unaware they still existed. Where does a person purchase such an article?"

"Amazon, Walmart, Costco, any electronics retailer…"

"Alright, alright. Why?"

"Because I'd like you to shoot the main attractions for us to review. Use your precious iPhone in most instances, but grab legitimate photographs of the highlights. Ironically enough…" Julie strolls to her desk, then fumbles through the drawer. She orbits waving a plastic card, and shrieks, "*Catch*," frisbeeing it my way. "A Target voucher containing approximately seventeen bucks. Put it toward a nifty camera strap to drape around your neck."

"You joking? Shall I snag a pair of Croakies to attach to my Oakleys while I'm at it? Bust out your rolodex and cough up the fax number for 1985 ASAP. What's your deal today, Doc Brown?"

"You'll also need a black Sharpie."

"And why on earth would I need that?"

"To write the date across the lower border."

"Ah, that explains it. Think you've jumped the shark, Fonzie."

"You aren't obliged if my guidelines trigger an uneasiness."

I sigh, then utter, "No, no. It's highly doubtful you'd proffer a solicitation without provocation, and I'll try my darndest to cooperate, hidden agenda notwithstanding. I just never imagined you for the sort who championed psychoanalysis."

"This fee..."

"Quid pro quo, Julie," I interject. She scowls, unresponsive. "Quid pro quo, Julie!" I reiterate sinisterly.

"Yes, Hannibal?" she urges exasperatedly, inserting an eye roll to communicate her disdain.

"My compliance is conditional."

"I'm waiting with bated breath."

"It's imperative you admit I'm your favorite patient."

She quells the impulse to laugh by biting her lower lip, but eventually relinquishes. "You're the bee's knees, the cream of the crop, the..."

"I detect a tinge of sarcasm."

"Very astute."

"Touché. And allow me to retort. You're the finest ambassador this profession has conferred."

"Flattery will get you everywhere. I beli..."

"Hang on, closing remarks."

"Proceed, counselor."

"From the bottom of my heart, merci beaucoup. You've saved me on countless occasions, and I'm lucky you're in my corner."

"Aw, that's incredibly sweet. I knew you had it in ya."

"You are the Morpheus to my Neo."

"And we're back."

"The Phil Jackson to my M.J."

"Er..."

"The Paris Hilton to my…"

"Time's up. Take a hike." I rise, smirking, and leave. "Hey!" she hollers, halting me in the foyer. "If you want to chat, I'm available. That doesn't mean I'll be there at the drop of a hat, but text me and we'll devise a solution."

I react somberly, laying the theatrics on thick with sniffles. "After all these years," Julie leaps to her feet, frowning. "I've finally…" Julie converges. "…worn you," Julie grips the knob. "…dow…" Julie slams the door in my mug.

FAR WEST TEXAS

Marfa's been on my radar since news of an art installation called Prada Marfa saturated the web. For starters, it's not an actual clothing outlet. Prada Marfa is a freestanding, non-functioning storefront built in 2005 by Berlin-based artist duo Michael Elmgreen and Ingar Dragset, who attest they envisioned it as a pop architectural land art project. Composed of a biodegradable, adobe-like substance, the sculpture was meant to slowly melt into the soil, representing a surrealist commentary on Western materialism. Contrarily, they outfitted the interior with authentic Prada apparel, entailing women's footwear and handbags, donated by Miuccia Prada herself. She even authorized usage of the company logo.

Many locals presumed the creators were corrupt, and the exhibit constituted glorified product placement under the guise of artistry. Several hoodlums took matters a step further and vandalized the premises, opening night: windows smashed, walls graffitied, and the space was looted. Elmgreen & Dragset repaired the whole shebang, installing reinforced glass and internal alarms to protect against future shenanigans. Additionally, bottomless purses and right footed shoes replaced the stolen wares. Following the overhaul, just a few fame-seeking idiots have defaced the property. At any rate, a fifteen by twenty-five-foot faux boutique in the middle of nowhere that's attracted esteemed photographers, social media influencers, and ordinary pedestrians for a decade and a half epitomizes something I must behold firsthand.

Whether this landmark opened the floodgates to tourism remains contestable, but the town is home to notably more. From the press I've read, it purports to baring astonishing architecture, contemporary museums and galleries, plus a collection of top-shelf hotels and eateries. Two of the greatest American-made movies filmed there, as well.

The George Stevens blockbuster *Giant* starring Rock Hudson, Elizabeth Taylor, and James Dean, shot its exteriors around Marfa. Although the A-list cast guaranteed success, the hoopla spiked through the roof in the aftermath of Dean's fatal wreck. When it premiered, fans and critics alike lavished rapturous praise upon the motion picture. *There Will Be Blood*, the Paul Thomas Anderson historical drama depicting the ruthlessness of capitalism during the early 20th century oil boom, which saw Daniel Day-Lewis earn his second Best Actor Oscar, documented the preponderance of its content on a ranch within spitting distance of downtown. Incidentally, the Coen Brothers' Academy Award-winning revenge thriller, *No Country for Old Men*, adapted from the Cormac McCarthy novel, recorded segments nearby, synchronous to *Blood*. That said, the meat of the production transpired in New Mexico, thereby disqualifying it.

However, the predominant item luring excursionists to this remote setting is the Marfa Lights. Without turning too *X-Files*, this mysterious phenomenon reportedly flourishes at dusk between Marfa and the Paisano Pass if gazing toward the Chinati Mountains. People travel from every corner of the globe to inspect. In 1986, the Texas Department of Transportation constructed a parking section to ensure vehicles didn't clog up the roadside. By 2003, legend grew so big that Presidio County intervened. Marfa High School students collaborated with TxDOT, designing a humongous viewing center for the public to employ. The Chamber of Commerce hosts a yearly festival commemorating the spectacle, to boot.

Accounts vary, but generally speaking, the lights manifest in various shapes and sizes, irradiating shades of orange, yellow, green, blue, red, or white. They change as they move, fuse together, split apart, then disappear. It began in the late 1800s after a teenage cowpoke named Robert Reed Ellison observed a strange glow while tending to a herd of cattle. He reckoned they were an Apache campfire.

That supposition was proven erroneous once the Apaches themselves made a similar observation, inferring they were falling stars.

Over one hundred years later, no scientific explanation persists. The most prevalent theory alleges the luminescence emanates from the headlights of traffic bouncing off the neighboring hillside. Yet these sightings originated in an uninhabited region virtually impossible to traverse by automobile, fundamentally invalidating the hypothesis. I've got a hunch it's that despicable Chupacabra stalking prey with a headlamp. Anyhoo, I aim to David Duchovny this bitch and find the truth, or at minimum, get super stoned and see what all the fuss is about.

MR. BRIGHTSIDE

It's a quarter past eight, and I'm practically humping the reception desk inside an upscale steakhouse, primed to wage war on the aloof hostess as to why my date and I haven't been seated. In a previous life, I'm certain I was a defense attorney. My propensity to verbally spar with anybody that challenges me is unprecedented.

The badge donned by this evening's opponent spells **JODIE** – chestnut bangs, navy blazer and slacks, temperament of a mannequin. From her RBF, I deduce she isn't in the mood to tangle with the current ordeal. Meanwhile, it's the apex of my day.

My companion perches atop a bench, quivering in embarrassment, fidgeting on her Samsung Galaxy. Peasant. Nonetheless, the wavy blonde locks, skintight gown more appropriate for summer than winter, toned gams, and heels are ridiculously sexy. Disastrously, the moment she unzipped her yap, I knew this wouldn't end well.

Amidst the jaunt from her apartment, we explored the core popular culture fields: cinema, music, and literature. She'd never heard of Benicio Del Toro or Michael Fassbender, yet firmly believes Selena Gomez should be allotted increased chances to spotlight her skills, and *Mean Girls*… that's her pride and joy. She worships Ariana Grande and RiRi yet seemed clueless to the likes of Jimi Hendrix or Elvis Presley and only discovered the Grateful Dead in the wake of John Mayer joining them. She positively adores the *Twilight* and *Hunger Games* sagas yet couldn't identify with *Harry Potter*, and on the subject of *A Confederacy of Dunces* or *Catch-22*… fuhgettaboutit. Her name's Becky – wait, maybe it's Karen. Who cares?

"When I make a reservation, I expect you to hold the reservation," I tutor.

Jodie gawks blankly. "We're doing the best we can."

"Hogwash. Confirming 8:00 implies that you'll show me to my table at 8:00 sharp. Not 8:01, not 8:05, not 8:10, not 8:15, but 8:00 and sooner if feasible. And by the looks of it…" I lower my inquiry to the IWC Portugieser Chronograph strapped around my wrist, "…it's 8:19 p.m."

"Sir, no offense…"

"My Spidey sense is tingling. There's a massively offensive remark forthcoming. Start over."

"Don't take this the wrong way…"

"Oh, I'll undoubtedly misconstrue it. Try again."

"May I ask you a question?"

"Sounds like you already did."

"You're a fucking asshole!" she broadcasts irately and stomps away.

"Jodie, come back! We were just getting acquainted," I rant acerbically. She doesn't abide. Alternatively, a bloke in his thirties, spray tan, bespoke three-piece suit, waltzes up, chortling derisively. He's the GM of the joint and an old chum, and Ethan's witnessed this demonstration often.

"Chased off another one, didn't ya?" he heckles.

"Is it my fault you hire nitwits that can't tell time?" I retaliate Socratically.

"Apologies, monsieur. The onus lies with me. Our asinine sous-chef needed reprimanding. Table for two?"

"Yeah, it's me and…" My speech terminates as I pivot toward Natalie – wait, maybe it's Maggie – and despite pleading ignorance to the existence of Elvis, she was apparently blowing smoke up my ass because The King, or Queen, rather, has left the building. "I'm rollin' solo. But do me a kindness and arrange a four-top, si vous plait. Going balls deep on a Wagyu Tomahawk with all the fixins."

"Anything for you, your highness."

"Grazie, my liege."

"How's the gig?" he prods, escorting me through the bar area.

"Livin' the dream, dawg."

"This kosher?" Ethan gestures at a booth, unveiling a stellar perspective of twentysomething vixens dressed to the nines in a bid to entice the bevy of investment bankers and car dealership owners into becoming their sugar daddies.

"Splendid," I endorse, sliding onto the leather.

"You're bringing me to The Killers next month, aren't you?"

"For the millionth time, yes. You've got such a boner for Brandon Flowers."

"He's the man! No pun intended," Ethan joshes, annoyingly referencing the band's megahit.

"Get the fuck outta here and instruct the waiter to fetch me a bottle of 2018 Austin Hope Cabernet Sauvignon and that seared ahi appetizer. And it better be comped to offset the unmitigated lack of respect I've endured from this establishment." Ethan and his shit-eating grin vamoose. I glance toward the entrance. The airhead's gone AWOL. Bye, Felicia. **Mental note:** create a Match dot com profile pronto.

A DAY IN THE LIFE

I work in music. I possess zero talent of any kind. I can't sing or play an instrument. I don't manage an artist or run a record label. I'm not even the person booking the concerts. My job ain't overly cool, and it definitely ain't glamorous; hence, there's no reason to elaborate. Then again, you're curious, so…

I supervise the formation of marketing collateral implemented to promote the ultraexpensive tours. The graphics blanketing Tame Impala's website announcing their upcoming dates. The cheesy radio advertisement publicizing Chris Stapleton's amphitheater engagement this *Sunday, Sunday, Sunday!* The television commercial during *Jimmy Kimmel* touting Billie Eilish's extravaganza at the basketball arena. The animated videos posted on Travis Scott's social media platforms hyping his impending global invasion. All me. Okay, technically, it's my "creative direction" that effectuates it, but the credit is mine and mine alone.

I'm the beneficiary of a gaudy business card, brandishing a hugely ambiguous designation adjacent from a distinguished corporate insignia that I flash whenever necessary. I'd be lying if I claimed I didn't get laid on the strength of it. See, I live in the Midwest, where true showbiz positions are few and far between. It goes without saying my craft has transformed me into a local celebrity. The populace conjectures I'm more prominent than I am by dint of having access to awesome tickets and occasionally partying with rock stars, which illustrate telltale signs of worth and distinction. And who am I to teach the plebeians they're mistaken? Besides, it isn't like I let it go to my head (insert winky face emoji here).

As suspected, the vocation doles out a fuckton of perks. The consensus crown jewel being the paid furlough we're allocated the final two weeks in December. I'm guessing delegates of the diversity and inclusion division met with the chief human resources officer, then she emailed the President, preliminary to him informing the CEO, and they unanimously concurred that since there were so many discordant faiths, and everyone feels compelled to act so goddamned PC, might as well grant the staff early parole for "good behavior." Supplementarily, it bolsters employee morale, and within an organization that grossed in excess of ten billion dollars the preceding fiscal calendar, they could afford it. Whatever the rationale, the benediction empowers my wanderlust across our great nation whilst obtaining a paycheck. Yahtzee!

AUDREY HEPBURN

Wednesday is considerably slower than anticipated. A larger part of the industry essays beating the hiatus to the punch. That's fine by me. It dispenses an interval to concentrate on stupendously urgent affairs, namely shopping. My dude, Spencer, asked if I'd meet him at the mall to collaborate in selecting gifts. There's a slew of stuff I should tie up instead, but I shelve the whole schmear.

First of all, I love to shop, yet don't have anyone to shop for. This characterizes an idyllic justification to peruse the markdowns and falsely front that I give two shits about others. Secondly, Spencer's also my mortgage broker and landed me a fifteen-year at three percent. He maintains I owe him. Last but not least, I really love to shop. Hey oh!

I spurn the infernal Salvation Army bell ringer en route to the food court and clock Spencer annihilating a Sbarro slice.

"Apweciate you bean hur," he mumbles, mouth crammed full of cheese and pepperoni. Spencer finishes chewing, then slurps his fountain drink and says, "I'm terrible at this rigamarole, and when it comes to material possessions, you're on par with a chick."

"That isn't a compliment, but I'll allow it. So, whose ass needs maximum kissing?" I pry.

"Jennifer."

"What's the budget?"

"Limitless."

"Holy Schnikes. Why?"

"Damage control. She found out about my Vegas guys' trip and had a conniption. Relatively confident she's on the brink of calling it quits."

"And you're of the mindset the right present will fix this?"

"Provided you do your duty properly."

"Then…" I break into chorus. "Heigh-Ho, Heigh-Ho it's off to Tiffany's we go."

"Brilliant."

Spencer and I walk and talk, elbowing through the hordes of consumers toward Holly's Utopia. "How bad did things get?" I interrogate.

"Bad."

"Like bad, bad?"

"Bad, bad."

"Like I lost my shirt playing poker or I awoke next to an overdosed prostitute?"

"Put it this way, between the craps tables, Zuma and Carbone feasts, plus a marathon at the Rhino, I dropped your annual loan payment in the span of forty-eight hours."

As Spencer pushes forward, I come to a standstill. After a couple steps, it registers I'm no longer by his side, and he curls around to locate me.

"Precisely how much you pulling down?"

"I'm keeping up with the Kardashians."

"Fuck me!"

"Shake a leg, princess. Maybe I'll nab you a spiffy trinket while we're at it," he antagonizes, adding a synchronized sneer and dismissive tushy pat.

We infiltrate the store, and I usher him to the vitrine. "What does she know?"

"Oodles."

"Well, don't forget, animosity is temporary, but Wu-Tang is forever."

"Thanks for those astounding words of enlightenment, RZA. Now, can you please just help me? It's dire straits, man."

A darling salesgirl, radiant aura, sneaks behind the display. "Hi, I'm Abby. Would you…?"

I heighten a finger to my lips, and she promptly hushes. "Abby, was it? Watch and learn, hon." I veer toward Spencer and motion at the showcase. "You see these cute open-heart earrings?"

"Affirmative," he responds, surveilling the merchandise.

"Those are for making a bonehead comment regarding her family." With our optics glued, I glide my hand along the glass. "See this mother-of-pearl wire bracelet in eighteen karat rose gold?"

"Aye, matey."

"That's for letting it slip she's packed on a few el bees." I cleave his arm and lead him to the edge of the cabinet. "But we aren't here for them, oh no. Take a peek at these diamond and ruby encrusted key pendants." He inclines to appraise, then diverts his contemplation reticently. "*This* is the bling a filthy rich buffoon buys his lady once she unearths the depravity his dumb ass embarked upon in Sin City."

We consult the winsome gem vendor. She nods repetitiously, simpering. Spencer whips out his Chase Sapphire and surrenders it.

"Be a dear and throw in the matching twenty-inch chain," I coax, sensually brushing the hair off her shoulder. Abby beams, snatches the card, and scampers away.

"For somebody who loathes this holiday to such a degree, you're truly a whiz," Spencer applauds.

"You've confused atoning for morally reprehensible deeds with Christmas."

"Explain to me again why you uncompromisingly despise it."

"What's that?"

"The birth of our Lord and Savior."

"Excluding my parents' fatality?"

"Yes, smart aleck."

"Where shall I begin? How's about the fact it starts earlier and earlier every year?"

"In what fashion?"

"By mid-November, entering a retail outlet, movie theater, or public restroom without some yahoo wishing you a '*Merry Christmas*' becomes unavoidable."

"So?"

"It's a superfluous month of cheeriness. Name another festivity celebrated for an entire thirty."

"Erm, uh…"

"Independence Day – one day. Veterans Day – one day. Memorial Day – one d… one weekend. Same difference."

"But it's Christmas."

"Yeah, and? Hanukkah lasts eight nights. Are Jews lighting the candles on the menorah and spinning dreidels four weeks prematurely? Nay. It's meshuggeneh."

"I have a funny feeling you've overanalyzed this."

"Just heating up, pally. Assuming you're driven to celebrate something at length, then why not a noble campaign? Breast Cancer Awareness for instance. You want more?"

"Nope."

"What about Black History? You realize 'they' intentionally gave that the shortest month. Racist!"

"Could we…?"

"Hold on, there's dozens."

"I'm begging you."

"Ever hear of Pride or Movember or National Pizza Month?"

"Enough alread… Wait, when's National Pizza Month?

"October."

"Get to the point for crying out loud."

"The *point* is that those signify meaningful events befitting an elongated celebration. Christmas totals a solitary day and a lousy one at that."

"Bah humbug! You're a bloody scrooge." He pumps his fist and, in his dopiest geriatric imitation, grumbles, "Get off my lawn, you damn kids!"

"Hardy har har. Changes nothing."

"Bro, you can't fabricate a single element that makes you jolly? Midget strippers wearing elf costumes? Spiked eggnog? Anything?"

I pause to ponder the inquisition. "Tell ya what, Charlie Brown, I'll ante up two. *Die Hard* and *Home Alone*," I avow apathetically to Spencer's bafflement. "If it wasn't for Jesus, then John McClane and Kevin McCallister wouldn't exist, and therefore, I'm eternally indebted."

Little Miss Sunshine revisits, dangling the tiny teal bag. "Here you go," she coos.

"Abby, thank heavens you're back. My friend has gone loco," Spencer opines jocularly, inducing an adorable smile to spread across her cheeks.

"Where's my cut?" I incite curtly, impelling her exultation to darken.

"Oh, um, we don't, ah, receive commission, sir," she stammers.

"Mm-hmm, sure," I gibe. With Spencer in tow, I trudge toward the egress and seconds before desertion…

"Merry Christmas!" Abby exclaims, stopping me cold. Spencer's unable to restrain himself as I steamroll past him.

WE ARE FAMILY

Every December, the parentals and I piled into the station wagon and set course for a destination. Ordinarily, we would voyage to Florida and bunk at my grandma and grandpa's Clearwater condo. Our clan resided in Toledo, Ohio, and The Citrus State is a straight shot down Interstate 75. We'd spend the evening at the halfway mark – Chattanooga, Tennessee.

Growing up, Mom and Dad didn't draw a ton of moolah. Resultantly, the cruddy "roach motels" we lodged at stemmed from necessity, not volition. It became a significant stumbling block between them. Money problems led to irritation, and altercations germinated, but the unbelievable thing about my folks – neither walked away angry. They had this uncanny approach to confronting these occurrences beyond comprehension. Undeterred by where, when, or why, one of them orchestrated a means to play their wedding song – Jim Croce's "Time in a Bottle." It served as an everlasting reminder to their commitment. Accomplishing this feat wasn't the easiest. Strangely enough, there was a day and age the internet and mobile phones were nonexistent, yet somehow they made it happen. Vinyl, cassette, jukebox, radio request, cd – come hell or high water – that ballad transmitted, and the lovebirds slow danced from beginning to end. A ceasefire bloomed, and the universe reverted to normality. Such unselfish dedication is inconceivable, particularly in this era of divorce. Their mutual deference constitutes the central ingredient for my interminable bachelordom. I crave what they had… or so I convince myself.

As the years ticked by, the old man's stock ascended, but he lacked the wherewithal to support us on his own. Inevitably, mom acquired part-time employment at her father's furniture store, handling the logistics and bookkeeping. During this chapter, my gramps continually offered monetary aid. Although the majority would've seized the charity, dad's dignity wouldn't approve of it.

That stood amongst a wealth of remarkable traits he sought to bequeath to his son. Personally, I've got zero qualms with handouts. Somebody wants to give me a leg up, fuck it. Mama ain't raise no fool. Having said that, I admired my father immeasurably and will attempt to instill his convictions in my progeny, supposing I sire any.

Eventually, he elevated into a senior executive, and she added saleswoman to her burgeoning résumé, and the dough finally began pouring in. From this newfound financial windfall, they bestowed a car on my sixteenth birthday. Fueling the tank and reimbursing them for the insurance fell upon me, however. It thrilled mom and dad to furnish the vehicle, but paying my dues was incumbent because they couldn't condone freeloading. So, ipso facto, I secured an after-school job at a baseball card shop, and we'd each joined the labor force, evolving into the picture of middle-class, familial happiness.

Over the last two winters of high school, we proceeded on our automotive adventures, and they even allowed me to participate in the planning. When I turned eighteen and went off to college, I'd outgrown vacationing alongside mommy and daddy and traded them for trips to Panama City and Daytona Beach with my peers. Post-graduation, we discussed the possibility of a reunion odyssey, but the occasion never arose.

Long story short, it doesn't take a shrink to decode the impetus behind abandoning my regularly scheduled programming and hitting the road is directly attributed to those journeys accompanied by the individuals who spawned me. What's the adage? The older you get, the more you become like your parents. We forfeit a substantial chunk of adolescence running from that concept. The burning desire to gain freedom emerges as an overriding concern. Then, somewhere down the line, you'll grasp how many items you condemned were for your benefit. And the extent to which you miss the times spent together, hoping they aren't too late to recoup. Grievously, in this circumstance, they are.

STARTED FROM THE BOTTOM

I debated dining in the presence of La La Land execs but bailed. My antipathy toward listening to tales of megalomania, followed by copious amounts of back-patting, took precedence. As a substitute, I'm rendezvousing with vaunted muckety-muck Patrick Montgomery, aka Monty, for digestifs at a local haunt of mine: cheap booze, cozy atmosphere, and a diverse crowd where everyone knows my name. He'll detest it.

Monty and I sat beside each other amid orientation and instantaneously struck up a friendship. He fantasized about prospering in "da bidness" and played the game the way it was meant to be played, sucking enough cock to further his career, but not so much that he lost every sliver of self-respect… just the bulk. Promotion after promotion ensued until he developed into Pollstar's Bill Graham Award recipient, thus, contributing papal supremacy. As we've uncovered, triumph in the domain of music accords impunity from the rules of decent society. Today, he's responsible for an ample portion of the highest-grossing tours across the continent. What's more – his gargantuan expense account exceeding the per capita GDP of Luxembourg. Typically, I'd exploit this, and we'd pop into a gentlemen's club, squander thousands on lap dances, and he'd write it off as client hospitality. Sadly, for my penis, I'm preoccupied with getting the hell out of dodge.

He texts to apprise he's delayed. C'est la vie. Mercifully, the corn distillation is fulfilling its prophecy. I'm parked at the counter, shooting the breeze with a group of homies from the neighborhood. The lion's share of my quotidian routine comprises upper crust snowflakes, whereas my confidants on this side of the tracks comprise an assorted lot: Blacks, Asians, and Latinos retaining distinctive backgrounds and socioeconomic statuses. The most valuable lesson my mother taught me – love all humanity. And while it's in vogue for Caucasians to trumpet that their clique integrates minorities, it's another thing entirely to actually hang out and regard them as equals. My ability to harmonize with people, irrespective of race, creed, color, gender identity, and sexual preference, emblematizes a criterion I'm tremendously proud of. There isn't an iota of hate in my heart toward anybody. Except vegans. I fucking hate vegans.

Anyhoo, these cats are captivated by my profession, standard of living, blah, blah, blah. They persistently ask tons of questions in relation to my glitzy M.O., but I elect to flip the script. I relish the opportunities I've been afforded, yet scrutinizing them is banal. Inexplicably, I feel hollow when weighing my position in the world at large. That being the case, I burrow into their aspirations and how I may be of assistance. Over and above that, I savor the camaraderie… in moderation. And if scoring drugs proves daunting, they're unfailingly philanthropic.

"Busy at the office?" my guy Jevon queries.

"Buried."

"On that trill shit?"

"Negative, Ghost Rider. It's the run-of-the-mill classic rock and country turds. As soon as the artists you're… Who you reppin' nowadays? A rapper that incorporates Lil or Baby or a weapon into their moniker?"

"I resemble a twelve-year-old white girl to you? I don't mess wit dem modern joints."

"A thug blazing a hyphen or acronym or dollar symbol or…?"

"You finished?"

"Yeppers. Oh wait, is it Adele?"

"I'm gonna toe tag your ass."

"Bahahaha! Educate me."

"I kick it old school. Gimme a splash of Stevie, Nas, Sade, Tribe, and I'm cool and the gang."

"Nice."

"I fucks wit Adele though. She tight."

"She's performing at Deer Creek in July. I've got a plus one. Interested?"

"Right on, G!"

"They treatin' ya okay at the brewery?"

"Quit that racket a minute ago. Busting ass for minuscule cash is criminal."

"Let me pull a few strings."

"Foreal?"

"Mos def. You're a hard worker, and just need to get your foot in the door."

"That's wassup."

"No sweat, J." I commute to Hector, a gifted urban street artist who hasn't reached his complete virtuosity. "Sup witchu foo'? Grinding?"

"It is what it is, player. I go with the flow."

"My offer stands. Whenever you're ready for a nine-to-five, I'll put those talents to use."

"Bet. 'Preciate it, fam."

I reconnoiter the posse. "You fellas thirsty? Shots and beers on me." They hail the supplication exuberantly. "Yo!" I bark, upward bob toward Sam the bartender. "Hook me uh…" As I'm tallying the quantity, a plethora of scoundrels cracks the procession. "Round of Fireball and PBRs." They express boisterously enthusiastic gratitude, and it leaves me warm and fuzzy.

"Where Mellow Yellow at?" Jevon grills Hector.

"Dunno."

"Who's 'Mellow Yellow?' " I extend to Jevon.

"Kim."

"Ooh-wee. Savage."

"Whatchu talkin' 'bout, Willis?"

"That's a gigantic Oriental slur."

"Pssh. You met Kim? He's a pothead. And he's Korean. Mellow… muthafuckin'… Yellow."

"Bazinga!" Hector snarls as they pound fists.

"Why you here on a weeknight, anyway?" Jevon presses scornfully.

"Catching up with my buddy from Los Angeles."

"He a douchebag like you?"

"Humph. That's an injustice to us douchebags worldwide."

Sam distributes the libations, and I propose a toast. "Good friends help you move. Great friends help you move a corpse. L'Chaim!" They chuckle, and we clink glasses, then guzzle the cinnamon whiskey.

"My brotha," rumbles an unmistakable baritone at my backside. I gyrate to greet him.

"Well, I do declare. If it isn't the venerable Patrick Montgomery, as I live and breathe. Gents, you're facing a genuine entertainment mogul. My colleague recently procured a mammoth 360 deal with Drake. He's helming the OVO empire." Monty doesn't blink. His air of superiority soars through the ether. Hector and Jevon bid me farewell and chaperone the entourage elsewhere.

"Still doing that?" Monty drills snootily, removing his overcoat and placing it primly around his stool.

"Doing what?"

"*That*," he expounds, motioning disparagingly toward the empties. "This rescuer complex you're saddled with. Socializing with everyone. Picking up the tab for everything."

"Consider it penance for a genetically clear advantage."

"Mm-hmm. Seems you're seeking absolution."

"I'm merely trying to do my part."

"By enabling alcohol abuse?"

"By subsidizing the underprivileged so they can engage in a little fun. I want to be a good person."

"You are a good person. Stop wasting your dinero demonstrating it."

"Luckily, there's plenty where that came from. And how would you know I'm a good person? You're an awful judge of character. What makes me a 'good person?' "

"This sort of nonsense. Your altruism is aggravating, Oprah."

"I prefer Bono."

"Riddle me this, Bono: ya think I'd bankroll a mob of penniless losers to win favor with the man upstairs? Eff that."

"If you don't mind me saying, you're an abysmal human being," I rebut contemptuously.

"Been called worse," he conveys, then skims the room. "You've brought me to a shithole," he proclaims in front of a passing waitress. "The night is young. Let's cop an eight ball and a coupla hookers and hightail it to my penthouse at the Conrad."

"God, you haven't changed a bit. Remind me why we're boys."

"Because I supply your life with meaning and I'm brutally honest for your own welfare."

"Sit your butt down and order a drink."

"One drink, then we're splitting." He settles in and waves at the bartender. "1942, neat," Monty beseeches as Sam stares, puzzled. "Clase Azul?" Monty canvasses.

"Are these brands of liquor?" Sam instigates blindly.

Monty huffs and puffs. "How 'bout Scotch? Glenlivet? Macallan?"

"We don't carry Scotch. How's Jameson?"

"Christ on a cracker. This is a bar, correct?" he contests scathingly. Sam glowers at me, implying I'm liable for Monty's condescending asshole skit. "Do you carry water and ice?"

"Huh?"

Monty gesticulates his fingers briskly, indicative of signing words, then speaks in a mocking timbre, mirroring a repulsive stereotype of the deaf. "Do you have frozen cubes of H2O and a faucet?"

"Um, yeah."

He lowers his limb and relapses to his default patronizing modulation. "Wonderful! Add a smidgen of both to the Jamo, numbskull." Sam scoots, and Monty turns to me. "Never again."

I pinch the bridge of my snout, dismayed. "What brings you to town?"

"Territorials' summit. The inner circle hashing out prospective touring lineups and timetables."

"Anything earth-shattering I should be privy to?"

"John Hancock an NDA."

"Hints, stat."

"On the record, it's the same ol', same ol'. Off the record, I'm drafting several loftier initiatives: reunite Zeppelin, a Daft Punk/LCD Soundsystem co-headline, assembling a 90s Seattle grunge package curated by Eddie Vedder. Ho-hum."

"Mazel tov, rabbi. I'm impressed."

"That's how I roll, bitch," he brags as his beverage surfaces. "Things copacetic in the marketing department?"

"Between us, I'm tired of it."

"Booyah! Welcome to the majors, meat."

"Excusez-moi?"

"You're joining my team. You'll be a sensational promoter, and moving you far, far away from this dump is critical."

"Indianapolis has grown on me. It's low-maintenance."

"Cut the shit. You bask in that whole big fish, small pond scenario. You're a cult hero to these retards, rendering the idea of relocation that much scarier."

"Fuck yourself."

"I'm serious."

"Fine. Recruit me, Saban."

"Putting me on the spot, eh? I thrive under pressure." Monty muses over his bribe. "Double your current earnings, and a corner window along with residency in perennial, eighty-degree temperatures, instead of this absurd frigidness."

"They're referred to as seasons, and I appreciate them."

"You'll forgive me if I choose a singular, tropical climate. And why are you even here? I thought you're from Ohio."

"Dad was transferred my freshman…"

"Fascinating. Defend the basis behind your branch existing in Indi-fucking-ana. The Midwest's a cesspool, but this state takes the cake. Perhaps I'll coerce the suits into bullying *you* to transfer," he clucks unscrupulously.

"Such a dick," I reply as Monty smirks in gratification. "Alright, hypothetically, I accept your proposition and migrate west. Then what? Forced to start from scratch. A factory reset, if you will. New digs, new…"

"Since when are you afraid of a challenge?"

"It isn't that it's… I've felt mighty bleak about our field lately."

"Oh, cry me a river, Justin. Spare me the pity party. You wanna boost your self-esteem, take a sabbatical and volunteer at Greenpeace or a doggy daycare. Grow a sack, ya pansy."

"Jesus!"

"Abrasive yes, but somebody hasta. I'm not one of your minions who licks your testicles and pretends they taste like vanilla ice cream." He gulps his concoction, then surveys mine. "Bottoms up, buttercup. If you're intent on behaving cunty, we'll cruise to my hotel. I imagine there I'll obtain a proper cocktail."

I capitulate, draining the contents, then summon Sam. "Check, please."

"My treat," Monty insists derogatorily, gloving his wallet.

"No, no. I bought a round for those honorable lads you so eloquently dubbed 'losers' and I'm quite capable of swinging yours, as well."

"Trust me, the finance nerds won't deny an extra hundred bucks for the future of America."

"Fair enough, Bezos."

Monty's archenemy reappears, and I bevel to my left. Sam sets down the bill and unwisely asks, "How was it?"

"Nauseating," Monty deadpans, then transitions into a frightfully bigoted Mandarin caricature. "Confucius say barkeep who doesn't satisfy parched customer deserving of castration." He dallies for melodramatic flair, sluggishly reinstating his hubristic intonation. "Sorry, mate, it's beyond my control," he counsels, slapping his Centurion AMEX atop the walnut without glimpsing the damage. Sam hoists his eyes and lopes off.

"You are a piece of work," I murmur to the conceited prick.

"Indeed," he acknowledges egotistically, slinking into his jacket. He rests his paw upon my collarbone, feigning sincerity. "Pay close attention. Your moral compass has always pointed in the wrong direction. The service we provide delivers euphoria to millions. Find solace there." He knocks my temple, then continues. "Get outta that head of yours. This business requires a different breed. Count your blessings. Everybody wants to be us."

"Did you just *Devil Wears Prada* me?"

"Damn straight. Meryl Streep's a goddess, and Anne Hathaway has an exquisite rack." He smacks me across the jaw. "Snare my stuff from the eunuch. I've gotta drop the kids at the pool and do a bump before we bounce," he promulgates, then swaggers indomitably toward the lavatory. "And no tip!" he clamors off-screen.

What a scumbag, but his unabashed arrogance is riveting. Truth be told, he molded some valid arguments. Maybe I'm beating a dead horse. Sam consigns the receipt and tidies up. Seventy-six measly dollars. Ah, heartland pricing. I shell out a fifty percent gratuity for bearing the brunt of Monty's jackassery, then pocket the plastic and paper. Adios, amigo. Uber awaits.

TRAVELOCITY

Once the site of my pilgrimage is locked and loaded, it's time to get down to brass tacks. Action item number one – prearrange a rental car. I'm the owner of a Mythos Black Metallic Audi A7, which the ladies have branded the "Batmobile," insofar as I'm Bruce Wayne behind the wheel. Or did I manufacture that epithet? Immaterial. The Audi simply isn't cross-country practical. And factoring wear and tear plus the depreciation you'll prevent on your personal machine generates a no-brainer decision.

At the outset, I reserve two classes of vehicles to cover my bases. Keep in mind, these agencies are like boxes of chocolates – ya never know what yer gonna git. Each encompasses various makes and models, and I demand options. There's a mental checklist of qualifications to address, and it habitually revolves around cognate components.

First and foremost – comfort. Sacrificing prolonged stretches within a confined area necessitates assurances of delight. Heated seats, sheepskin upholstery, and bountiful trunk space depict upgrades I jones for. Next is gas mileage. The farther I can drive without filling up, the better. Technological advancements such as satellite radio and GPS aren't an issue if you're dealing with reputable merchants, yet it'd stink to ascertain your wireless battery's fading and USB ports weren't installed.

I'm a comparison shopper and scour gobs of apps to root out the best bargain. I've also wrangled a pirated index of corporate discount codes, and I cannot tell you the regularity whereby I've had to persuade the agent that I'm a tax consultant at Pricewaterhouse. I'll gladly garment tweed and bifocals to save ten percent.

With transpo clinched, I segue to accommodations. Nothing says R&R in the manner of a sumptuous hotel. Numerous constituents compose the perfect stay. What size is the mattress? Which amenities are provisioned? Where's it located in proximity to the excitement? When's last call? Am I able to steam or sauna? Piss off, I'm a bougie S.O.B.

I'll devote weeks researching to certify the savviest determination gets made. I surf the property websites, read as many reviews as possible, and scroll through scads of photos. Ringing the concierge isn't a hindrance either. It's basically a full-time gig.

And just so you're up to speed, I don't subscribe to that private home rental malarkey. Airbnb, Vrbo, or anything else connected with boarding at a stranger's abode is downright outlandish, both as a guest and host. Leasing a dwelling over an expanded term – tenable. Permitting total randoms to sleep in your bed for coin – sheer lunacy.

I institute a Google search for MARFA HOTELS, divulging half the candidates involve camping or RV parks – fat chance. Some people revere nature – not me. I deem myself a great indoorsman. As a matter of principle, I refuse to attend Bonnaroo, and I'm VVIP. Correspondingly, I've nixed the famed El Cosmico, Marfa Yacht Club, and the equivalent on the grounds that snoozing inside an Airstream, tent, tepee, or yurt ain't my thang. Upon closer examination, it's apparent my choices entail The Hotel Paisano, The Lincoln Marfa, Thunderbird Hotel, and Hotel Saint George.

Paisano's the most recognized of the batch, seeing that it sheltered the cast and crew of *Giant*. What's unusually intriguing is their home page reveals you can rent the "James Dean Room," advertised as the quarters where the infamous lothario slept. I'm a staunch admirer of the cultural icon from Fairmount, Indiana, but the debauchery perverted fanatics have consummated between them walls must be abhorrent. Moreover, the decor looks too archaic for my tastes. Images of the floral-patterned quilts, shabby carpeting, and antique wooden desks and dressers scream granny to me. In fairness, I belch similar drivel about the Waldorf Astoria, and that franchise exemplifies dignification.

The Lincoln and Thunderbird seem comparable and très swank. Renovated with the stylish frills poseurs (i.e. the author) covet: stained concrete flooring, contemporary furniture, and communal courtyards for reveling. The cherry on top – they border the town's points of interest.

Then there's the Saint George. A scan of Yelp and Trip Advisor are all that's needed to corroborate this is the place I belong. Situated a block from the main drag, it flaunts those newfangled indulgences I lust after. The room description stipulates tall ceilings, free Wi-Fi, locally crafted furnishings, remodeled bathrooms yielding luxurious apothecary products, and plush spa robes and slippers.

The downstairs unveils a hipper than thou gastropub aptly titled, Bar Saint George, featuring a daily happy hour that punctuates a spicy margarita and charcuterie platter. Their spirits inventory underlines a gamut of tequilas, bourbons, and vodkas. The menu accentuates a breakfast burrito, smoked brisket mac and cheese, and meatloaf. Pow!

LaVenture is their gourmet restaurant, and the initial web result pledges the noun being of French descent, translating to "a nickname for a lucky or fortunate person." Result numéro deux denotes an individual who "enjoys change, travel, and new experiences." Regardless of the definition, their cuisine sounds delish, exposing dishes ranging from blistered shishito peppers and crispy brussels sprouts to an eight-ounce filet and pan-seared sesame tuna. The lobby harbors the Marfa Book Company, stocking regional publications, artwork, and paraphernalia. It duplicates the caliber of trendy literary shop you'd encounter throughout Shoreditch in London or on Manhattan's Lower East Side.

Despite a steeper fee than my alternatives, it oughta be worthwhile for this all-inclusive trophy. I compare their rates against the booking apps and net a nominal abatement at Hotels dot com. **Legal disclaimer:** Marfa will become the least industrial locality I've ever visited, nullifying the customary reduction I'd accrue from my bogus jobs at Goldman Sachs, Deloitte, and Microsoft.

BOYS DON'T CRY

A lone day prevails until I'm gone like the wind. At the moment, I'm booked solid with staff meetings flanked by my administrative committee. Five of our elite convene around the oak conference table, evaluating a laundry list of topics.

Three hours later, the natives are restless. I resolve to ordering food so they can regain their potency. Chinese represents the desired nationality, and P.F. Chang's delivery arrives in under forty as we recess for lunch.

I boot up the tube. TNT's televising *Shawshank Redemption*. There's a sprinkle of motion pictures I'm willing to suffer through censored profanities, veiled nudity, and tedious commercials. This bides at the forefront. It showcases two of the preeminent acting portrayals captured on celluloid, and Frank Darabont's screenplay derived from Stephen King's novella is ofttimes depressing, ofttimes heartwarming, but unfalteringly magnificent. **Mental note:** investigate driving to Zihuatanejo, Mexico, next year.

As I'm constructing a chicken lettuce wrap, Morgan Freeman's celestial vocals recite the immortal soliloquy, decreeing you should get your ass in gear or get your ass in the dirt. Shortly afterward, he clumps along the sand toward his pal Tim Robbins, crouched atop his moored boat. Their pupils link, and they shimmer with glee. Tim disembarks, and he and Morgan cuddle affectionately to conclude the masterpiece. Mid-bite, a noise mimicking a canine whimper emits across the slab. Steadily, I heft my faculties to discern Marshall, head honcho of our video squadron, bawling shriller than a toddler. I fling the appetizer onto the plate and glare at him.

"Are you fucking kidding me?" I ask.

He pivots from the TV and wipes his saline. "What?"

"Whaddaya mean 'what?' You're crying."

"I'm not crying, you're crying."

"Nice comeback."

"Blow me."

Jesse, my senior graphic designer slash teacher's pet, pours salt on the wound. "You kiss your brother with that mouth?" he rags, then winks at me in self-exaltation.

"Fuck you dudes. You've never cried watching Shawshank?" Marshall opposes, fluctuating his gaze between Jesse and me.

I rise, then distend my waistband. "Would you look at that? No vagina."

"Cold-blooded," Ralph, our dipshit, online developer who I resent unreservedly, grizzles. **Postscript:** Ralph was foisted upon us by the sponsorship division, and the bureaucrats eschew terminating him because his aunt's boyfriend's cousin is related to Madonna. Trollop.

"What about *Rudy*?" Marshall tenders.

"Rudy who?"

"*Rudy*, Rudy!" he squeals. "The movie where the guy defies the odds by making the Notre Dame football roster."

"Yeah, c'mon man," Ralph interjects. I mull the repercussions of punching the schmuck. "During the finale, when his teammates chant his name, and the coach subs him into the game for the only time in his collegiate career."

Marshall hijacks the reins. "Then he sacks the quarterback, and they cart him off the gridiron on their shoulders while the stadium cheers. Bullcrap that didn't stimulate tears."

"First things first, fuck Notre Dame," I propound.

"Excuse me, Mister THEE Ohio State University," Jesse obtrudes snidely, citing my alma mater. Now I yearn to feed him *and* Ralph knuckle sandwiches. His stint as the apple of my eye is kaput.

"Goddamn right. Go Bucks! And screw those Irish Catholic bastards."

"Hold the phone, I'm Irish Catholic," Marshall avouches.

"Then screw you too."

"I went to Michigan," Ralph briefs.

"Whoop-de-do."

"Buckeyes versus Wolverines. It's the biggest rivalry in sports."

"Nuh-uh. They haven't been relevant in over a decade and won't unless they cheat, so shut the hell up."

"Cold-blooded," he asserts yet *again*. Doofus commands the originality of *Taken 2*.

"As I was saying, prior to Ralph rudely interrupting… It's Hollywood. Familiar with the phrase 'creative license?' There isn't a prayer that shrimp transforms into a Fighting Leprechaun and goes out in a blaze of glory."

"You insinuating *Rudy* is a lie?" Jesse probes.

"I couldn't care less about *Rudy*. Quit changing the subject. This discussion hinges exclusively on Marshall's menstrual cycle," Alexander, the audio supervisor, cackles in the corner. He's assumed the pole position. Jesse can bonk himself.

"Okay, what does make you cry then, stud muffin?" Marshall pesters.

"Did you just describe me as a 'stud muffin?' "

"Embarrassing slip of the tongue. But answer the question."

"Nada, ya homo."

"You expect us to believe you don't cry at all?" Jesse pries.

"It's a grim reality. For reasons unknown, I'm unable."

"Seriously?" Ralph oppugns.

"Scout's honor. I possess emotions; however, the capacity or reflex that triggers a physical reaction doesn't endure. Even after my parents died."

"That's messed up," Marshall pronounces.

"So you've never cried?" Jesse disputes.

"No, I purely can't recall the last time it occurred."

Alexander breaks his silence. "That's tragic, bub. And not to belittle the situation… I heard through the grapevine you're a colossal rom-com fan."

"What?!" Marshall blares at the top of his lungs. "And I'm the homo?!"

I fleer at Alexander. "Thanks, bro."

"You're welcome."

"Alexander's humiliating revelation is accurate. There's undeniably a place for romantic comedies in this calloused heart of mine."

"Oh, then, without a doubt, you've wept like a bitch," Marshall denounces to everyone's amusement.

"If memory serves… the closest I've succumbed to sobbing was… *Notting Hill.* When Julia Roberts tells Hugh Grant…" I clear my throat, then raise the octave of my inflection to a higher frequency, emulating the pretty woman. I enunciate woefully, stopping and staring at each of them in turn. As I recount the yarn illustrating how the planet's most renowned actress implored the lowly, travel book-selling Englishman to fancy her for who she was on the inside rather than the outside, a placidness suffuses the room, climaxing with my cohorts welling up. "God, you're a bunch of sissies. I'll finish this myself. Gather your grub and bugger off," I ordain, routing them toward the exit.

"That film is divine!" Alexander spiels. A trickle drips down his cheek.

I scoff farcically. Peeping at the end of the table, I discover Ralph shoveling Mongolian beef into his piehole.

"Why are you still here?"

"I'm starving and…"

"GET THE FUCK OUT, RALPH!"

"Cold-blooded."

STEVE JOBS

A calendar reminder pops up, alerting me that my year-end review with iTunes is pending. I activate the Do Not Disturb on both the landline and Instant Messenger, hover the mouse over the musical note in the dock, and click.

As far as I'm concerned, nothing's as invaluable to a successful four-wheeled outing than in-vehicle entertainment. Thoroughly comprehending Spotify has conquered the globe, I'm partial to curating my own catalog and having everything at the touch of a button. Which, in essence, outlines Spotify to a tee, but I'm old-fashioned. Therefore, I expend redundant man-hours organizing my playlists. I've been fiddling forever. Today I'll apportion the undivided attention it so richly deserves.

I dissect the template into five categories:

ARTIST – No one listens to every musician whose MP3s inhabit their hard drive. Consequently, I go to painstaking lengths guaranteeing my favorites are easily accessible. From Sinatra to Ocean, The Stooges to Queens of the Stone Age, Eric B. & Rakim to A$AP Rocky, Chet Baker to Kamasi Washington, and all dope songsmiths in between. If you're charmed enough to come onboard, then a customized folder you shall inherit.

SINGLES – Characteristic of your average middle schooler, I'm addicted to a mainstream chart-topper. I haven't downloaded the Biebs' or Miley's entire discography, but I sure as shit bought "Baby," and "Party in the U.S.A." plus zillions of additional radio bangers.

GENRE – Sometimes the mood warrants EDM. Others mandate 60s R&B. Whatever the allocation, it's sorted and prepared to launch.

MISCELLANEOUS – A denomination consolidating specialty items that could theoretically procure independent headers, yet don't. Stuff in the vein of the soundtrack to *Miami Vice* and classical compositions including Beethoven's *Moonlight Sonata*, conducted by the Boston Philharmonic Orchestra, populate this realm. It's a long shot I'll cue up any of these. Nonetheless, you can't predict when you'll be haulin' ass, impersonating Sonny Crockett, and attain an irresistible urge to pump a little Jan Hammer through your speakers.

DAVE GROHL – He's hands down the greatest human in the history of mankind; thus, anything he's written, recorded, or produced garners a directory unto itself.

Vocational "emergencies" aside, it takes roughly ninety minutes to lay out the whole megillah squarely how I want. I plug my iPhone into my MacBook Pro, and the two innovative objects work their magic in swift precision. Upon ejecting the device, I engineer a supplemental analysis to verify the files slotted properly and grow psyched for my fast-approaching escapade.

IRON MAN

I've still got an occupational obligation to tend to before I pack. Black Sabbath has invaded Indy, performing on their third "final" tour. Their reformation paralleled solely by Kiss, Eagles, and Motley Crüe for most occasions to call it a day previous to returning, again and again and again and...

One of my pro bono clients is a budding punk blues trio from Clarksdale, Mississippi. They're tonight's opener, and I promised I'd put in an appearance. Truthfully, I almost ducked out, but it's friggin' Sabbath. Also, there's a possibility of rubbing elbows with the Prince of Darkness himself, and that's a prospect way too supercalifragilisticexpialidocious to rebuff. Fingers crossed.

I sidle up to the arena at 7:30 p.m. and palm the security booth officer a Jackson, furtively authorizing my underground penetration. I don't mingle with the commoners, and I won't park near their hoopties. After hastening through the metal detectors, the overzealous, venue rent-a-cops momentarily detain me. The second I brandish my 'do you know who the fuck I am' credentials, they scurry away in search of a surrogate victim. I perambulate the restricted corridor, then flounce into the green room.

"There he is!" roars front man Jordan Neal, slouched atop a nylon sofa, tuning his Gibson 335. "Didn't think you were gonna grace us." He plunks the guitar and springs to his feet.

"No chance I'd miss this… Where's Ozzy?"

"That's your true motivation for being here, innit?"

"I'm appalled by the accusation. Came to watch you fools. Best damn band in the land," I aver, pausing to exchange grins. "Where is he though?" The coterie erupts into hysterics as I make the rounds, fist bumping the drummer and bass player, high-fiving the tour manager, and leering creepily in the trajectory of three platinum-haired groupies.

"How you doin'?" I ask the gals, deploying a spot-on Joey Tribbiani impression. It's repelled with a collective groan. Sluts. They reprise their TikToking or Tindering or LinkedIning.

"Hungry?" Jordan delves.

"Do wannabe rock stars don leather jackets, skinny jeans, and beanies?"

He peers at his PETA-illicit coat and nut huggers while readjusting his knit cap and yaks, "You brought jokes."

"Never leave home without 'em."

"Well, Seinfeld, there's pita chips, veggies, and hummus here, and catering's down the hall. Help yourself."

"Fan-freaking-tastic! When are you on?"

"8:00 sharp," his handler reports.

"Wicked. Couldn't be happier for you, bud. Sabbath. Epic, my friend."

"It's a dream. The shows have been killer, and the audiences dig it."

"You meet them yet?"

"Nope. Hopefully soon. Tommy and Geezer hide in their dressing rooms, and Ozzy... Ozzy's a hologram."

"HA! I wonder if he's..." I'm disrupted mid-sentence by an eerie British accent.

"Hello, children," the mystic figure vociferates, materializing out of nowhere.

"Jesus Christ!" I screech, caught off guard. We dart our appraisal in unison.

"Not quite," he squelches menacingly.

The Batman looms in the entryway, arms spread wide, suggestive of indoctrinating a congregation. His disheveled mane, medieval shillelagh, and all black everything attire echoes the Redeemer's Luciferian twin.

The throng is mute, gaping at the Godfather of Heavy Metal. He begins to chatter incoherently. Jordan slings me a sidelong glance, and I wince, indicating I haven't the slightest clue what's happening. Literal gibberish spurts from his maw. It's tantamount to exploring China sans translator. Ozzy doesn't cease mumbling as time seemingly freezes. A deep, bellowing laugh resonates, then crickets. Nobody flinches.

"Hey, Mr. Osbourne," Jordan replies demurely. "I wanted to say we're so appreciative for you inviting us. It's such a privilege. Told Joseph yesterday…" He delays, curving toward his percussionist. Whirling back, he finds the legendary singer has disappeared, as quickly as he emerged and in a similarly cryptic manner.

"What the frak was that?!" I appeal emphatically. The troupe hoots in merriment.

"Some trippy shit," a Barbie behind us yaps.

"Rock and roll!" Jordan hypes. He straps the six-string to his chest and strums a chord.

The production manager storms in and heralds, "Five minutes 'til showtime, chaps," then flees.

"We doing this?" Jordan posits to his rhythm section. They nod agreeingly and strut into the auditorium. Jordan bird-dogs me and asks, "You're coming, aren't ya?"

"Hells yeah!"

"Sick! You can stand onstage, or roam around, just steer clear of Sharon," he notifies, gleaming his pearly whites.

"Dealio," I rubber-stamp, tagging along sprightly. Fuckin' A. Monty may've been correct from the jump. My life's rad.

THE ESSENTIALS

Prepping for the road signifies a grueling exercise, albeit an inordinately enjoyable segment of the groundwork. I'm a clothes whore who owns more crap than Imelda Marcos. Most ex-girlfriends felt inadequate beside me in view of my keen fashion sense. Duh. Midwestern women and preening blend like oil and water.

Tom Ford embodies my style guru. Problem is, despite drawing a generous salary and being Tom Ford-cool, I'm unequivocally <u>not</u> Tom Ford-wealthy. That's why *my* style falls somewhere between 80s drug dealer and hip-hop pioneer — visualize *Less Than Zero* James Spader meets Run D.M.C. Levi's, Adidas, and AllSaints are my go-tos. I do, however, boast a smattering of Tom Ford accessories and ready-to-wear for after-hours parading. But I digress.

Implementing this each year allows me to assess my wardrobe and banish duds I regard as expendable. I then donate them to Goodwill. And we aren't talking about a fraying sweater or outdated fad. Naw, I donate designer brand staples and thousands of dollars' worth at that. Warren Buffett ain't got shit on me!

If you separated my closets, you'd distinguish two clashing subdivisions. The left engrosses articles I scarcely trot out, yet can't bring myself to relinquish: tuxedos, dress shirts, trousers, and a truckload of neckties. The right constitutes my everyday garb chock-full of button-downs, hoodies, and henleys. A compressed cluster makes the cut. Then there's my dresser. This encloses the necessities: undershirts, boxers, socks, denims, sweats, and tees. The core of what I'll adorn nest here. The coatroom is strictly for outerwear: trenches, puffers, sukajans, parkas, fleeces, peas, et al. Certainly toting a couple dependent upon the weather forecast. Which leads us to my shoe palace, teeming with footwear.

Oxfords, tennis, basketball, sneakers, and boots live like kings in their IKEA castle. Sad to say, only a few prestigious pairs will undergo the fortuity of strolling the West Texas streets. **Addendum:** Entombed beneath the planking resides my deadstock vault, duly baptized "Paolo Nutini" – IYKYK. Jordans, Dunks, and AF1s that'll never see sunlight but comprise my scion's inheritance. I've omitted the Yeezys I auctioned off to fund the trip.

I'm arranging for a five-day trek. I don't futz around on these quests. You won't catch me dropping by the World's Largest Ball of Twine or the Cabazon Dinosaurs. I progress from point A to point B with an eye toward investing as long as possible, wherever I'm headed. Accordingly, my itinerary allots for one day to reach Marfa, two days to lollygag in town, and another day for the ride home. I earmark an extra day to be safe.

In terms of packing, I conform to the regulations chronicled throughout the movie *Up in the Air*. Travel light, travel smart, appoint a versatile ensemble, and stow it efficiently to maximize space. Granted, George Clooney was flying, so he avoided checking luggage, yet the same overarching theme applies. And I have leeway since I'm able to hang belongings I'd rather not iron inside the automobile. Furthermore, it features a trunk that I prohibit from congesting should I accidentally flatten a hitchhiker. Where else would I stash the carcass until there's an opportune juncture to bury it in the woods? I'm teasing… or am I?

Taking these determinants into consideration, I assemble a pragmatic compendium of threads for any affair and potential climate change within my Tortuga Outbreaker backpack. Meanwhile, I crate a heap of unwanted clutter. I'd approximate the impoverished receiving a donation valued at six grand. That's the sum I'll claim on my taxes, at least. On to sustenance.

My YETI Tundra cooler proves optimal to stockpile with refreshments. I snap up a surplus because pulling off for meals is acceptable but frittering gratuitous intervals perusing gas stations for drinks and snacks is inane. Bottled waters, sugar-free Red Bulls, and canned Starbucks Nitro Cold Brews reign supreme. A growing boy's gotta nourish, so hard-boiled eggs and individually wrapped cheeses will tide me over between restaurant sit-downs. Toss in a bag of ice, and it's raring to go.

Every now and again, I gits a lil' white trash and amass a treasure trove of NASCAR-endorsed junk foods: Jerky, Combos, and Moon Pies. I incorporate a mixture of protein bars, gummy bears, and enough Tic Tacs to disburse unbounded minty freshness. Lastly, no excursion's complete without cigarettes. Although I shun inhaling the butts the way I used to, three packs of Parliaments are as requisite as food and beverage.

I fill the container, schlep it into the garage, where it'll refrigerate overnight, then prop the goodies and cancer sticks atop the lid. Bedtime. Just shy of twenty-four hours before my getaway gets underway, and the real world is in the rearview.

CANUCK SYNDICATE

I revive around 9 a.m., grab a shower, then climb into my indie chic uniform: Mack Weldon sweatshirt, Vuori joggers, Alpha Industries bomber, and limited-edition Stan Smiths. I bolt by 9:20 a.m., and I'm behind my computer ten minutes later. Got a jam-packed agenda consisting of virtually no professional duties.

Between 9:30 and 10:00 a.m. I'll respond to emails and voicemail messages. "Get Michael Rapino on the line, chop-chop!" typifies an edict I reap extreme jubilation yelling into the hallway willy-nilly to keep my underlings on their toes. He's the most powerful man in the biz. I know him. He doesn't know me. We met once. He called me Timmy and strode away. It's my crowning achievement. Well, that and the time Irving Azoff gave me a shoulder massage, which remains an altogether different and profoundly unsettling story I'm not at liberty to discuss.

Immediately succeeding, I shall police my hired guns to ratify matters are functioning smoothly. In the region of 10:30 a.m. I'll double-check my TripTiks to reinforce I haven't missed anything. I'm conceivably the sole person under the age of senile who prints directions, documents, even coupons. I adopted that from my father. I'm unsure why, but it furnishes a queer contentment. Full transparency, I rarely resort to the printouts, given they're digitally embedded on my cell. That's impertinent. It's an homage to youth when conditions were drastically harder for everybody.

At 1:00 p.m. I've designated an hour intermission. Winners don't take lunches; they merely block off periods geared toward sex or errands. It's crucial I stop by a CVS. There's something oh-so arousing about travel size toiletries. Apart from collecting the rental, there isn't a whole lot in limbo. Goodness gracious, great balls of fire! **Mental note:** set fantasy rosters and survivor pool selections. Catastrophe averted.

WHITE IVERSON

My sliding office door is a metaphorical turnstile, with people coming and going around the clock. The show kicked off through an unannounced visit from my ex, Vivian. 'Twas exceptionally thoughtful of her to deliver my personal effects eight months post-breakup. She's presumptively been super busy. Here's the play-by-play: Viv barged in, flung the box at me, flipped the bird, then evacuated. The Gucci loafers I wore to her sister's wedding are MIA. No worries. I'll acquire them anew via Poshmark. Credit where credit's due – the Ziplocs of feces were next level.

The current occupant – my dear friend Matthew Nathaniel, he of the two first name variety. Our fellowship born from a shared affinity toward Humphrey Bogart films, F. Scott Fitzgerald rhetoric, and top-grade sushi. He surprised me with a much-needed care package containing prescription uppers, counterbalancing Vivian's defilement.

"Godspeed, old sport," Matthew confers, shakes my hand, and skedaddles.

Not long after, my PA Ashley bursts in. "Can you…?"

"I beg your pardon. Did we forget how to knock?" I taunt. Ashley flashes me the stink eye and retreats. She wings the panel, then pounds the glass intensely. "Who's there?" I ask with the uttermost flamboyancy.

"Can you approve these Post Malone ads?" She plonks a stack of papers across my desk, and I critique expeditiously.

"For fuck's sake, is it me, or has he gotten more face tattoos?"

"I think he looks hot," she weighs in thirstily.

"Of course you do, ya hussy. And tell the dorks they nailed it," I spout. She gloms the samples and tries to sneak away. "Yoo-hoo! We aren't done here yet."

"Ugh! What?"

"Patience, young grasshopper. Good things come to those who wait," I presage, fanning an envelope to and fro. She rips it from my mitts and snickers. "Your efforts don't go unnoticed. Mahalo. Have a fabulous break."

She upheaves the flap, abstracts a cashier's check, and radiates with jaunty astonishment. "$2,500?! Holy shit!"

"You've earned it."

"You're the best!"

"Preach. Now begone."

Ashley takes a couple of steps, then coils. "And Merry Christmas!" she yodels. My teeth clench, skin tautens, while I chew over reclaiming the bonus. Fortunately for her, she splits and secures the pane.

My replica Richard Mille confirms it's a quarter to four, and I'm ahead of schedule. Rent-a-car here I come. I didn't pick Enterprise connoting they ain't picking my ass up. If only I could finagle a patsy into chauffeuring me. And BAM… Jake, our rotund multimedia animator, serendipitously shuffles past. Christopher "Jake" Jacobs and I are bosom buddies. He's also my flunky du jour, a laurel requiring him to do my bidding. Sucks for Jake. **Sidenote:** Mr. Jacobs freelances as a magician. When the fella infiltrates a shindig, the females, the mirth, and the narcotics vanish entirely.

"Jake, a moment," I petition domineeringly. I perceive he's drawn to a halt narrowly beyond my field of vision, contemplating whether this is job-related or a recreational invitation. Slowly but surely, he reverses, clicks his heels, and twirls, then walks plumb into the Windexed glass. He bounces off and wobbles dazedly. Seconds later, he straightens himself and enters as though nothing happened.

"Sir, yes, sir," he salutes.

"You intoxicated, soldier?" I inquire by virtue of his recent mishap. Plus, it's commonplace to get tipsy during the final day. And in summation, Jake's an alcoholic.

"Sir, maybe sir," he slurs, grinning like a tubby kid on Halloween.

"Slug an espresso, junior. You're following me to my pad to unload the Audi, then giving me a lift to the rental agency."

His vitality evanesces. "Dude!" he yowls, then lowers his voice to elude the threat of Big Brother's espionage. "I downed two Jäger bombs, umpteen Jack and Gingers, and burned a j at the luncheon."

"Weren't you the hooligan that chugged five rounds of Tito's rocks with a cocaine chaser then drove us to the casino Saturday?"

Jake grimaces confoundedly and ripostes, "Well yeah, but… Cocaine."

I shrug, escorted by a simultaneous neck tilt. "Can't argue with that rationality. You're shuttling me, nevertheless. Fetch your keys, son."

"But, but…"

"Respect my authority!"

PASSPORT TO ADVENTURE

Home is a few miles from headquarters, which, as it turns out, is a few miles too many for Jake to be operating a motorized vehicle. The galoot wasn't fibbing. He's three sheets to the wind. His busted 2002 Subaru Forester's gently swerving and getting honked at half a dozen times to stay in its lane. I should feel guilty… Muahahaha! We access my driveway, and I motion for him to exit. He rolls down the window, smoke billowing.

"Wassup?" he asks.

"Beat it. I'm the captain now," I dictate, declining to ride shotgun with a sloshed motorist. Reluctantly, he unfastens his safety belt, then dawdles around the bumper. "And eighty-six that cigarette," I rib.

"Not a cigarette, muchacho," he clarifies as I wriggle inside. The stench of weed so pungent I've obtained a contact high.

"Jesus, Cheech!" I squawk. He chortles, tokes, then snuffs the roach into the blacktop.

Amidst our exodus, he cranks the volume on some hippie jam band garbage that makes my ears bleed and flails his appendages sporadically, to the extent I speculate he's having a seizure. I switch to the alternative rock channel, and Kurt Cobain causes him to cramp. Speaking of Nirvana, I wish Jake smelled more like Teen Spirit than the rancid Patchouli scent oozing from his pores. Out of my peripheral, I track his pinkie inching toward the knobs and whack it. We eventually agree on Howard Stern.

"Refresh my memory about your holiday plans," I canvass.

"Fort Myers. My folks sublet a condo along the beach. A little fun in the sun, then Big Apple bound for Phish at MSG."

"Have a blast, compadre."

"Thanks, brosef. You gonna reveal the location of…?"

"No way, José."

"D'ya honestly think if you leak this confidential tidbit, I'll blab?"

I scowl at him. "Yep."

"Oh, please."

"Fine, but so help me God…"

"Mums the word." Jake puckers his lips and twists the imaginary sealant.

"Marfa."

"Where in tarnation is that?"

"Tejas, twenty hours west of Indy."

"Bloody hell. You don't go stir-crazy? I'd lose my shit."

"I love to drive," I submit, perception welded to the boulevard. "The peaceful and calming properties epitomize the polar opposite of my rigorous routine. And unbeknownst to you, getting there is practically impossible unless you're Jay-Z and Beyoncé and PJ into Marfa Municipal. Otherwise, you're hopping commercial flights to El Paso or Austin. They're both hundreds of miles away, and it's unrealistic I'd depart either upon touchdown.

"This works like a charm. Should really take my mind off things. As lame as it sounds, I could use some self-care. Listen to tunes, see the sights, unwind, and recharge the batteries." I curtail my garrulous oration and anticipate a reply. Instead, a loud snore expels. Jake has conked the fuck out at 4:20 p.m. in the passenger seat of his own jalopy. Pathetic.

I park and traipse into the dealership. There are three partitioned kiosks, each staffed by highly divergent characters.

To my left, a ravishing millennial evocative of a *Cosby Show*-era Lisa Bonet. She's a fox. I'm frazzled even peeking at her. Focus on the task at hand, moron.

Bozo in the center strikes me as the stereotypical jock that sidestepped electing a major because… sports. He skated by and graduated summa cum dimwit, but who's got time for an education when you're D-1 varsity, and before long, 'seeking energetic team players to join our squad' seems like a chance to keep the glory days alive until you realize you're manning a shift at the local Hertz, bunking in momma and dadda's basement. Wow, that was cruel. He's probably a spectacular human.

Starboard produces a follicly-challenged elder – cardigan, paisley bow tie, khakis, and beige wingtips. How's he not retired? Perhaps his Social Security wasn't cutting the mustard. Didn't he propagate offspring that would subsidize the…? Why do I give a rat's ass?

A deduction of mega-significance is inescapable. Pinpointing the most vulnerable salesperson spells the difference between nabbing a BMW 330i and compromising for a Nissan Sentra. As I rotate across the triumvirate, sniffing out the mark, an acute unease pervades me. I'm hastily metamorphosing into the gawking wacko by his lonesome. Stall dammit. In short order, I unsheathe my iPhone and simulate conversation.

The fogy ventures to oblige. "Sir, can…?" I elevate my forefinger, conveying I'll commune with him soon, then turn my back. Must act PDQ! It's a foregone conclusion they'll grow suspicious and form a coalition against me. Breathe in, breathe out, breathe in, breathe out. Eye of the tiger.

I abort my fraudulent confab and spin toward the pensioner. He's deserted his cubicle. I hypothesize that his bladder defeated him. Old fart oughta wear a diaper. Veering to the meathead, I theorize he's playing tic-tac-toe predicated on him trash-talking his monitor. "Tic-tac-toe, bitch!" Dummy's oblivious to my existence.

Swiveling farther, I espy the foxy lady smiling coyly. Our irises entwine. Zoinks. Timidly, I glint behind me to establish what she's observing. Bupkis. As I confront her scrutiny de novo, the smile has broadened. She beckons me, and I obey like the pitiful male I am.

"Whatchu scheming, Slim Shady?" she pokes humorously.

I lay my license atop the ledge. "Who to brownnose for a complimentary upgrade," I confess.

"Should've chosen Brandon," she flogs, stealthily nodding at the nincompoop. "You're definitely his type."

"Fuck my life," I blurt, provoking a healthy giggle from my newest crush.

She inputs my details, and her brow furrows studying the results. "Says here you made two reservations. How come?"

"Argh, I forgot to cancel one. It's standard procedure that I book a midsize and an SUV. I can't decide which class I want prep…" It sinks in I'm rambling, and I pipe down. "I have issues."

She scoffs, maintaining an ultra-seductive visage that renders me weak in the knees. "I'll try my best. Preference between them?"

"Whatever's clever."

"If you're coveting the sedan, I may be of service. But if the sport-ute is non-negotiable, I'm reduced to a Toyota RAV4 or Hyundai Tucson. There's a million families renting for the holidays, and many of the larger models are unavailable."

"I throw myself on the mercy of the court, your honor."

"You traveling alone? Peeped somebody with you earlier. By the way…" she peers at Jake's dormant anatomy, drool dribbling onto his shirt. "Your homie might've croaked."

"Ah yes, that's my pal Bernie. I'm crashing at his bungalow this weekend," I jest. My elation withers once I glean her befuddlement, noting I've referenced a flick feasibly ten years older than her. "It's just me," I acknowledge, dejected. "Why you asking?"

"Well, presuming constricted storage doesn't pose an obstacle, get ready to celebrate. I'll void the other booking and… ta-da. Had some big swinging dick return a Mercedes CLA this morning. Wasn't slated for another week. Luxury coupe at the cost of a Chevy Malibu, alright by you, Lone Ranger?"

"Right as rain."

"Marvelous. Go ahead and insert your card into the reader. Leave it in till I tell you to pull it out."

"That's what she said," ejaculates from my chops as horror spreads incontinently. "Such a douchey force of habit."

"You're something else. When prompted, sign the contract, then initial the next page if you're waiving the insurance." I assent. "*Now* remove your card," she adjures. "I suggest we check the exterior before I send you packing. After you."

"Whaddaya take me for madam? I'm a mensch. After <u>you</u>."

"Praise the Lord, chivalry isn't dead."

I trail ogling her caboose, urging me to accelerate. She inspects the Benz for glaring dings and dents. I should inspect the Benz for glaring dings and dents also, yet I continue to fixate on her impotently.

"Everything hunky-dory?" she examines, figuratively catching me with my pants down.

"Totally," I jabber posthaste, nescient whether or not this machine has four tires.

"It's all yours. Be careful."

"Careful is my middle name," I protest as she lofts the fob skyward. It caroms off my fingertips and plummets onto the pavement. She titters dubiously, then sashays away. Diarrhea of the mouth transpires again. "Hey!" I woof at her, and she pirouettes. "Are you a music fan?"

"Why?"

"Any interest in accompanying me to a concert?"

She vacillates, pondering the proposal. "Which concert?"

"I'll get us tix to anything you desire," I vouch pompously, believing my game is strong.

She approaches and calls me on my bullshit. "Let me guess, you're in the 'industry' and assume you'll dazzle the naive car rental chick by flossin'."

"No, I…"

"You'll scoop me up, whisk us to an outrageously priced dinner, then we'll saunter into the joint like royalty."

"Er, it's…"

"And as the attendants squire us toward your suite, they'll fawn over you, and I'll become so starstruck that diving into your bed afterward will be inevitable. Amirite?"

Oh Mylanta! She's on the precipice of repossessing the Mercedes and sending me back to the land of domestics. Why couldn't I keep my trap shut? I've got zero shot with this babe. Stupid therapist stuck in my cerebellum.

"Here's the deal. You're insanely attractive, and I'm super single. Eek." Dolt! Chill, chill, chill… "Okay, mulligan… Even though you're clearly out of my league, I felt there was some sorta vibe between us, and that going on a date sounded nice. I apologize for overstepping my boundaries. Disregard it," I cave. She eyeballs me silently. The interlude's excruciating.

"Too late. You offered." She withdraws, then cedes her business card. "Besides, I saw your email in the system. You thought I upgraded you because you're charismatic?" she roasts. "I'll consent to you wining and dining me to repay this huge favor."

Casting my optics at the glossy identifier, I beam zestfully. Her name is Zoe. Her fucking name is Zoe!

"What about him?" she quizzes, signaling at Jake.

Uh-oh SpaghettiOs! Que será, será. We aren't busy at the office, and I sincerely doubt anyone notices. "Stake me a twenty-four-hour head start, then inform the po-po," I lark.

"You never divulged your destination."

"Marfa. It's a town nobody's…"

"Give a shout to Hov and Bey for me."

"How did you…?"

"Not just a pretty face," she contributes wantonly. "Arrivederci, playboy." And with that, my future ex-wife bats her mascaraed lashes and dips indoors. I jizzed in my pants, literally.

Plumped within the cockpit, experiencing an irrepressible state of ecstasy, Ice Cube raps through my cognitive boombox as I reflect upon this felicitous Friday. Scored a date with the sexiest Hoosier I've encountered in ages, snagged a Mercedes Benz to tour America, and I'm on the verge of navigating toward my Holy Grail. Today's been a good day! I push the automatic starter, and the engine fires up. German elegance at its finest. We're gonna learn what this puppy has under the hood. Rushing back to initiate Instagram stalking is of monumental priority.

QUEENPIN

What's customarily a low-key scene has devolved – it's a shitshow. There's an assortment of adult beverages, mixers, and personnel strewn everywhere.

"Hello? Hello? Anybody there?" Allison, the receptionist, babbles into the wrong end of the receiver, crinkling a red Solo Cup.

"Yo, bruh," Jason, the shipping clerk, mutters, vape pen implanted, atomized THC spraying out of his schnoz.

Our CFO's lying down on the job, unconscious atop a couch, disposable wine goblet loosely suspended, pinot noir spilling onto the rug. "Sixty-nine!" she squalls, rousing from her coma, in all likelihood answering an unsolved accounting quandary or orgasming with the abetment of a smoldering, erotic compulsion.

This is an HR nightmare.

I take a lap to affirm my subjects are lucid. Most seem inebriated, and the halls reek of booze. Fuck this. I hotfoot it to my room, get comfy in the Herman Miller, and open The Gram to hunt for bikini pics of Ms. Zoe. On the cusp of turning freaky, her majesty intrudes.

"How we lookin'?" my skipper vets. She's ruled the roost across the last two decades, braving the heyday of sexual harassment in a profession built on loathsomely misogynistic behavior, rising through the ranks until reaching the pinnacle. Legend has it she blew Jackson Browne backstage at a folk festival, but that hasn't been formally substantiated. Anyhoo, the woman's a devout proponent of mine. Despite my parents perishing antecedent to my tenure, she's abreast of the circumstances and always remained extraordinarily respectful. And that's the solitary reason I won't advise her to diddle herself so I can snoop tantalizing photos of the rental hottie.

"Just checked in and cleared for takeoff," I perjure a wee bit. "You flirting with closing early, or ya wanna tough it out? I'm dandy either way."

"Let's wait fifteen, then I'll alert the troops. Cool?"

"Cool beans," I spoof, surmising we're finished. Consummately contradicting my hopes and dreams, she advances and yanks a decorative parcel from behind her heinie.

"Merry Christmas!" she howls.

"Very frickin' funny," I retort. She's keenly aware of my hatred toward the expression. I mutilate the Yuletide covering to denude a cardboard box stamped Amazon, encasing a paperback entitled *100 Things to Do in Texas Before You Die* alongside gift cards to Starbucks, Nordstrom, and, lo and behold, Target.

"Figured you'd profit from these on your trip."

"Well-played. Top-notch, top-notch. And I'll read the manual while I'm driving."

"Don't you dare."

"I keed, I keed."

"Better be. I need you in one piece. You're indispensable to this company and to me personally."

"Could you repeat that?"

"Kiss my grits!" she razzes. "On a serious note, you deserve this downtime."

"Thank you. When's Mom arriving?"

"Tomorrow afternoon. Ole Caroline's been counting the days. We weren't able to get together as frequently as I would've…," she clams up, posture modifying into sad resignation. "I'm sorry, I…"

"No harm, no foul, chief. It's incredible your mother's still kicking. Wish mine was too." She projects a melancholic mien, and I react with a contrived grin. "Cherish it."

"I shall. When are you hitting the bricks?"

"Power nap, then I'll jet. I conquer a sufficient amount at night. Less cars to combat."

"You and that Marfa, boy. Bring me back a souvenir this time, motherfucker!"

Her eloquence induces a snort. "I gotchu, boo."

She hugs me, then vacates. I lunge for the cellular, but in a tick, she resurfaces. "You seen Jake? I can't locate him anywhere."

"Uh… sure haven't."

"Goddamn slacker," she gripes, dashing down the passageway.

Whoops, poor Jake. Bummer. I thrust the gift cards inside my Ekster Aluminum Cardholder, then gander at her magnanimous travelogue. Pfft. Into the recycling bin it goes. What did she mean by, 'this time?' "Bring me back a souvenir <u>this time</u>," were her precise words. And then she alluded I'm an incest participant. It's a peculiar request on innumerable levels. She knows Marfa tops my bucket list, and I'm fairly positive I've purchased her a chintzy knickknack from every crusade – a thermos, magnet, or koozie, at minimum. That's disheartening. Prime example of early-onset dementia. The silver lining is once she's constrained in the assisted living facility, they'll promote me to CEO! **Mental note:** splurge on an indelible present. It's plausibly her swan song.

WARHOL

As the Herculean, crimson and white bullseye dawns, I reckon it's now or never to administer the preliminary phase of Julie's assignment, 'cuz there ain't no big-box retailers in Timbuktu. I enter the lot and jockey into a spot reserved for expectant mothers. I'll only be a minute, and they shouldn't be out shopping anyway.

"Camera aisle?" I ask a vested employee stocking tampons.

"Try F13," he replies, wielding the vampire plugs to guide me.

Bewitched by the carton, I agonize over buying one for Marshall. 'Tis mildly inappropriate, seeing as I'm his superior, combined with being an elementary school prank. But it's outright hilarious, and I'm an infant. In the end, I veto the whim and proceed.

The photography section contains dual styles of Polaroids. I compare the descriptions, opting for the Originals OneStep+. At my rear, a shelf staging numerous, polychromatic film packages affiliated with my nominee. Who knew this regressive technology would encompass such a medley? I extricate the Color i-Type, 5-pack bundle. Odds are there won't be nearly that many wonders to shoot, yet I haven't used a Polaroid in eons, so I'm bound to botch something up.

The decrepit hag at checkout scans and bags, then transmits I owe $219.13. Good golly, Miss Molly, that's highway robbery. It's defensible that my medical insurance should reimburse me. It was doctor recommended after all. Quibbling is trivial and launching an assault toward somebody knocking on heaven's door appears irresponsible. I remit the vouchers, pay the overage in shekels, and twenty-three skidoo.

SPOKEN WORDS

The office is closed. Although the putrid odor lingers, the staffers don't. Evidently, Lumbergh sent the memo, and everyone flew the coop. I too wanna make like a shepherd and get the flock outta here, but there's a final item to tackle.

They say audiobooks are the crux of any lengthy journey. I find them terribly hit-or-miss. When the stars align, a tale portrayed through your car stereo can culminate in time zooming past. Naturally, it begins with the manuscript itself, yet a multitude of external factors might spoil the foray. Envision Charlie Day narrating *The Catcher in the Rye*, applying his obnoxiously squeaky pitch. Holden Caulfield wouldn't have stood a chance. The mere thought riles me up.

It's incomprehensible how often I've discontinued an audible after a single chapter due to the voice-over actor's intolerance. The exclusive proviso more deplorable than an Anglo gent sustaining a deviated septum is an impassive British dame. That's extrapolated from personal inclination, versus sexism or xenophobic prejudice. I'd slit my throat if I had to hear Judi Dench drone on incessantly, thus precluding works penned by an English scribe. Apologies, Daphne, Virginia, and Jane; condemn thy publisher.

Also, certain novels aren't cyber age compatible. Listening to *The Grapes of Wrath* or *1984* or *To Kill a Mockingbird* contrasted with absorbing the printed text seems unimaginable. All that miraculous storytelling and imagery could've evaporated. So, whereas I'm not averse to downloading a few sonic fictional narratives, I'll never consider anything of substance excluding Kerouac's magnum opus – the Gospel for every traveler. Therefore, choosing entertainingly simplistic authors a la John Grisham and Taylor Jenkins Reid follows the path of least resistance. No disrespect Johnny and Tay Tay, you're stupendous writers, but I'm emphasizing my point. Allocate a first-rate legal thriller or tawdry scandal that keeps me on the edge of my seat while piloting the sterile dust bowl known as Kansas, and I'm aces.

Hurriedly, I select a Gillian Flynn, an Elmore Leonard, and fraternal twin Blake Crouch titles. And recognizing the census data tabulates Hispanics represent seventy percent of Marfa's population, I grabbed *Spanish Survival Phrases* weeks ago. I've been practicing somewhat and I'm grasping the lingo muy rápidamente. "Dónde está el baño" and "chinga tu madre" will doubtlessly come in handy. I receive an email confirmation and forward the invoices to the boss' lieutenant. Are these expensable? I'll classify the verbal literature as research and the español lessons under south of the border client relations.

I ram the laptop and charger inside my Tumi, pluck an envelopes and Sharpie from the desktop organizer, then take a parting glimpse. Hasta la vista bebé.

FIENDS WITH BENEFITS

The blaring ringtone propels me off the mattress at 9:30 p.m. I bathe to scrub the rust, and once I'm washed, dried, and dressed, it's 9:45 p.m. I swallow a 30mg Adderall, corral my backpack, then move toward the kitchen.

"Hey there," a sultry voice purrs. I totter backward and drop the Tortuga on the ground.

"Judas Priest! Scared the piss out of me," I shriek to the arrestingly, gorgeous creature docked atop the buffet, sipping champagne from a flute.

Darby is my ride or die. We met through a mutual acquaintance that fixed us up, thinking we'd be perfect for one another. Unfortunately, we were a tad too similar as she's, more or less, my female counterpart, yet much, much hotter.

She possesses those intrinsic attributes I told Julie I sought in a prototypical mate. Principally the boobs. Great boobs. A handful of dates later, we determined plutonic partners in crime opposed to romantic companions was win-win. We've been Bonnie and Clyde ever since, minus the armed robbery.

"See you haven't wasted any time popping the bottle of Veuve I've saved for a special occasion," I quip satirically.

"This *is* a special occasion. You're bailing, and I get your crib all to myself. Wanna bang?"

I'm barely awake, hyperfocused on my departure, and exorbitantly accustomed to her banter, so it doesn't impact me. It's unrepentantly who she is and how she speaks. The paragon of the modern woman. A whip-smart, statuesque brunette commanding the mouth of a sailor and an 'I don't give a fuck' attitude. For better or worse, she's the singular individual I trust to house-sit, fully apprehending the food and alcohol currently inhabiting my cupboards shall be gone upon my return. The alcohol, in any case. Broads displaying hourglass figures won't eat the groceries bachelors accumulate.

"Stellar idea. Shtup my bestie, then drive halfway across the country. I'll fall asleep instantly."

"Quit being a pussy," she comments, vaulting onto the porcelain and scraping her impeccably manicured nails along my neck in a method that would incapacitate most men. "May as well blow your wad before pulling over and…" Darby exhibits her patented devilish smirk.

"And?" I ask curiously.

"The cat's outta the bag, handsome. I've heard the rumors. Guys copulating inside rest area bathrooms. No judgment. Sounds fun if that's what floats your boat."

"That's supposed to be a secret. You aren't allowed to peek behind the curtain, Dorothy. And FYI, you are correct, so belay your attempts at luring me into hetero intercourse, harlot! I must conserve my strength for truck stop anal."

"Lame."

"P.S. I'd contemplate letting David Beckham and Brad Pitt touch Mr. Holmes."

"Those lucky ducks," she jives. "So, what's the plan, Stan? Heading directly to… where again? Martha?"

"Yup, I'm on my way to the Vineyard. There's nothing as invigorating as an island off the coast of Cape Cod during the dead of winter."

"Shush. The town's called…? Marcia? Marva?"

"Marfa. It's in Texas. We've discussed this."

"No shit, Sherlock. I'm messing with you, but the fact you're ditching me is annoying. Why can't you stay or travel somewhere warm or exotic? I'll take PTO and we can explore Savannah, Charleston, or anyplace aside from that hipster paradise of yours."

"Maybe next year. I've got to do this."

She sighs heavily then responds. "Promise me something then. Whatever happens, you'll come back as you are."

"Dafuq does that…?"

"Just promise."

"I don't understand."

"Just fucking say it!"

"I promise, good grief," I acquiesce, perplexed by the sullenness. She bows her skull, eyelids adhered, and there's a semblance of grave concern flourishing. I tack my thumb underneath her chin and raise it to equal mine. "Look at me." She balks. "I said look at me." After my second entreaty, she complies. "I'll be back in a flash, and we'll talk and text constantly.

"Plus, we're hanging New Year's Eve, right?" She bobs in approval. "Scope the parties, and I accord you carte blanche, provided we skip the masked orgy this go-round, Kubrick." She simpers, then snuggles me, squeezing tighter than normal. It feels amazing. Admittedly, it feels so amazing that I briefly debate accepting her salacious overture. Alas, I'm on a timeline and disengage. "You okay?"

"Yes, asshole, I just care about you. Now scram and hurry home."

I snatch a leaf of paper off the credenza and delegate it to her. "I guarantee you've memorized these, but you're an expert on how OCD I am. Garage code, alarm code, the number to 911," I chaff. "Keys to the Batmobile are in the drawer. Cleaning supplies are in the pantry. Do not have sex in my bed! I'd prefer you didn't escort any dudes here whatsoever, but God forbid you meet Ryan Gosling or Ryan Reynolds or some Ryan 'Big Dick' at the clurb, use the spare. Conversely, if you hook up with any chicks, then mi casa es su casa. Please remember to press record on the camcorder in the closet. Capiche?"

She laughs, ushering vivacity into her cheeks. "Capiche. Keep me posted and send lots of photos. Love you."

"Ditto." I smooch her, ensnare the backpack, and slip out. She stands in the doorway as I reposit my baggage. We trade affectionate mannerisms, then I wiggle inside the vehicle. Wending down the street, I witness her waving, gradually diminishing until she disappears altogether, and my maiden voyage to Marfa commences.

RUNNIN' DOWN A DREAM

I actuate the Waze app and disable the 'avoid tolls' feature because I like to live dangerously. Fees be damned! Distance and duration are what's pertinent. Collectively, I'm spanning 1350 miles over an estimated twenty hours. Add a couple hours for fuel, urination, and nourishment, and we're up to a double deuce. But I gain an hour trekking from eastern to central time zones, hinting that a 7:00 p.m. Marfa arrival is doable.

I'm starting along 70 West, then transitioning onto 55 South through St. Louis, preceding the I-44 merger. Piercing the Texas state line routes me down agricultural farm-to-markets, which connects with Interstate 20, where I'll whoosh past the *Friday Night Lights* towns. After encountering signs for Fort Stockton, I negotiate two-lane highways henceforth.

It's a steadfast tradition to inaugurate every road trip with my most beloved album – *Grace* from the transcendent Jeff Buckley. Tragically, not unlike so many of my idols, he was taken too soon. Awaiting incoming bandmates to rehearse his sophomore album, *My Sweetheart the Drunk*, Buckley drowned in the Wolf River on the shores of Memphis. A year postmortem, an unfinished compilation showcasing demos and abandoned studio tracks were released as a sketchbook depicting what the future once held.

The moment those hauntingly tortured vocal cords soar on the leadoff "Mojo Pin," my degree of tranquility challenges the Dalai Lama. I torch a Parliament, crack the window, and exhale. When the entrancingly forlorn "Last Goodbye" streams and his slide guitar intro fills the interior, my smile grows. I boost the decibels to eleven and speed into the dark.

CROWN OF THORNS

The mundanity of my surroundings is tiring, and the amphetamines are wearing off fast. I toyed with an audiobook before discovering, two chapters in, I'd already watched the movie adaptation. It's the critically acclaimed cliff-hanger revolving around a girl who travels by train and fakes her own death intending to frame her husband, except the chicanery goes awry so she and her fellow housewives push him down a flight of stairs, then she revisits her hometown to report about a serial killer whilst swigging vodka interminably, however, in a dramatic twist, ascertains that not only is her half-sibling the evildoer, but their mother also poisoned her late, genetic sister, which spurs her developing agoraphobia, and gazing at the neighbors nonstop. The New York Times extolled the novel as a "roller-coaster joyride tugging at your heartstrings." Goodreads reviews averaged four point eight stars. To tell you the truth, based on the speck I caught, David Fincher's version proved decidedly more enticing.

Steering toward Effingham, Illinois, amends the boredom forthright. Just north of the 70 and I-57 interchange, a cringeworthy monolith arises – A 200-foot-tall landmark christened **The Cross at the Crossroads**. This ain't my first rodeo with the religious monstrosity. That said, I suppress the evidence until it's staring me in the face. The gales are ferocious, and the chassis trembles as I strangle the wheel, yet the structure refuses to sway an inch. A cross doesn't necessarily signify Christmas, but it does symbolize mortality – to me and the Man from Galilee, justifiably. Conceding an endeavor at evading all elements associated with the holiday, or the Jewish carpenter, is futile, given I'm traversing the Bible Belt amid December, it's still premature to meditate upon the expiration of my kin.

My distraught mentality craters me into a surly mood. The APA's prescribed cure – a profane dosage of Rage Against the Machine and Kendrick Lamar. Each became the mouthpieces for separate generations irked by political and social malfeasance, corporate greed, and widespread pessimism that permeated their everyday lives.

Zack de la Rocha's subversive lyrics, blended with Tom Morello's incendiary riffs, were a ticking time bomb of discontent. Intuiting the band's aggression might've originally been conceived to impart a voice to the voiceless, the melodic nature of their ire resonated amongst multiple societal sectors. It's undisputable that Public Enemy, MC5, Fugazi, and KRS-One poured gasoline on a nagging, visceral inferno. Howbeit, no musicians sold anarchy to the masses like Rage did.

At some stage in the rap game, the genre softened. Unpredictably, a kid straight outta Compton rolled up and lobbed a Molotov cocktail at his adversaries. Following the lead of heroes N.W.A., Tupac, and Notorious B.I.G., Kendrick's parables were archetypes of unabated poetic indignation. The chameleonic cadence, the ingenious and topical rhymes, the unrivaled flow straddling imperiously unorthodox beats brought the menace back to an abnormally conservative ilk.

Shuffling through the jams "Killing In The Name," "Swimming Pools (Drank)," "Bulls On Parade," "The Blacker The Berry," "Testify," and "HUMBLE." galvanizes my disposition, and I jiggle my noggin unrelentingly. Thus, any susceptibilities I was repressing nimbly fade.

THE WASTE LAND(S)

I've swung by The Lou previously, and the tank's a third full, denoting a detour is unwarranted. And if the not-so-subtle racism of *National Lampoon's Vacation* has taught me anything, it's that you don't exit the freeway at this metropolis, or you'll wind up in the hood and locals will pilfer your hubcaps while doling out crummy directions.

Over the horizon, I descry the famed **Gateway Arch**. Despite the absence of light, the elephantine monument looks glorious. As I clasp my cell and aim through the windshield, the stainless-steel stunner turns translucent, and I tap the shutter continuously. Executing this in the midst of driving isn't the easiest chore, but I'm the iPhone Annie Leibovitz.

On deck, two disturbing, albeit absurdly amusing, billboards. **Uranus Fudge Factory and General Store** confectionary vows **THE BEST FUDGE COMES FROM URANUS**. Gee whiz, that's astonishingly distasteful… yet comical as hell! The ensuing advert presented by a Baptist church advocates motorists should **LET JESUS INSIDE YOU**. Hmm, I'm on the fence. Whereas my guts are tickled pink, the G-O-D and I retain quite the love-hate relationship. It's imprudent to ridicule his son with a thousand miles unresolved. The measure of havoc he's capable of wreaking would be unfathomable. What's irrefutable – the sponsoring ministry desperately needs to enlist proofreading services.

Pressing forward, there's diddly-squat worth mentioning until breaching the Red River boundary. The bloke who nicknamed Missouri "The Show-Me State" could've been a distant cousin of mine. That echelon of oxymoron entailed superlative cynicism even a cynical rascal such as myself is ill-equipped to yield. Unless he meant "show me the fucking way outta here." With reference to Oklahoma's "Sooner State" moniker, that incontestably sprang from somebody who drove, end to end, and concluded they'd rather leave 'sooner' than 'later.'

Nonetheless, both states share an enthralling attraction – a convenience chain denominated **Kum & Go**. I'll profess I'm the antithesis of a pundit on what defines civilized decorum. All the same, I know better than to designate any enterprise *"Kum and Go."* Wait, scratch that. It's a phenomenal brothel slogan! **Mental note:** analyze franchising costs and how hard it is out there for a pimp.

DEEP IN THE HEART

Accessing the great state of Texas, everything seems different. I flip on the hazards and veer off the pavement. Perched atop the hood, I quietly mop up the setting. I'm not the type of person to dispense particular consideration toward the simple pleasures the Earth offers, but I can assimilate the magnificence. The grass is greener, the air smells fresher, and as the clouds glide through the undiluted cobalt sky overhead, I begin relishing in satisfaction. Precisely the condition I've been craving – peace. A single week to offset the other fifty-one laden with mayhem. It all starts now. I reoccupy the Mercedes and forge onward, ecstatic.

I rove from I-44 onto Route 277, and the panorama shifts. Barring the occasional ranch, a herd of cows grazing the pasture, and several **WHATABURGER** restaurants, there's nullity. Although effervescence is sparse, it's as if I've become one with the universe. Am I so shallow and narcissistic that I've failed to question what else exists out here? Maybe I'm destined to reside beyond the big-city buzz. And right on cue, I streak by a tribe of goats and cackle hysterically, immediately returning to my senses. Welp, that was short-lived. I'm an ignoramus.

While I have reception, I ring Darby to notify her I've crossed the border and my anal virginity perdures. In response, she divulges the liquor cabinet's vacant, and she hosted a ménage à trois. That lady's a keeper.

DESCANSOS

A deluge of commemorative markers revering the departed embroider the highway. Every few miles, a pristine crop sprouts. I've observed these in various parts of the nation, yet never to this extent.

"Watch out. Vehicle stopped on shoulder ahead," forewarns my robotic navigator.

I catch sight of an unpopulated, vintage Ford pickup. There's a doddering gentleman bent over in a clearing, toiling with an obstructed entity. Ordinarily, I wouldn't give it a second thought, but my shoe involuntarily wills itself to the floorboard, necessitating me to skew onto the berm.

"Could you use a little help?" I examine, narrowing the gap between.

He kneels in frustration and squints into the daylight, assaying to identify the silhouette. "For the life of me, I cannot git this gosh darn thing upright," he apprises, employing a thick drawl.

"Mind if I try?"

"Be my guest."

I hoist him perpendicularly, then appraise the intersecting timber. The spray-painted inscription specifies the name **ANDREA CARTER** and phrase **FOREVER OUR PRECIOUS R.I.P.** I'm mesmerized.

"That's my granddaughter," he discloses. "Celebrated her seventh birthday recently."

"What happened?"

"She'd been ridin' the brand-new bicycle her grandmother and I bought her. Andi had a playdate a stone's throw from my boy's residence. He advised that gal to avoid th... Don't matter. The damage is done. Cops calculated the sumbitch was doing ninety. They found her mangled two-wheeler beside them trees, and her body..." He chokes up, speech adjourns.

I lay the memorial on the turf and stride toward the senior. Devoid of any rational explanation, I extend my upper limbs around him. His cranium slumps against my deltoid, and he weeps profusely. Ultimately, he detaches, wiping the dampness.

"Would you look at me? Crying in front of a stranger."

"Nothing to be ashamed of. My sincerest condolences to you and yours."

"You're an extremely compassionate young man."

If he only knew. I reconfigure the memento and hammer it into the soil, mustering every ounce of brawn within. "How's that?" I ask, receding to admire the fruits of my labor.

"Real nice. Real nice indeed. All that's missing is her portrait, but the goddamn Department of Transportation doesn't condone it."

"Well, it's a wonderful tribute, regardless. You build this yourself?"

"My wife and me. Despondency has relegated her to our bedroom. Hasn't left in days."

Criminy. What an ordeal. Do more for them. A scenario of this magnitude lodges outside my wheelhouse. That's not to say I haven't patronized the disadvantaged. Usually, it's at arm's length, though. Someplace allowing me to pretend I've made a difference without getting my hands dirty. Now's the time to put up or shut up. Is money the solution? Replacing the loss isn't attainable, yet I'd suspect they'd benefit from the endowment. I dig into my pocket, and he grips my wrist firmly.

"Don't even think about it."

"Please."

"No, sir. Your generosity's contribution plenty," he edifies, relinquishing his hold.

"How can I aid further?"

"There's some flowers in the flatbed. Lend me a hand?"

"I'd be honored."

We retrieve the bouquets and arrange them along the periphery. He gestures in esteem at the outcome.

"I oughta shove off. Still a ways to go."

"Where ya headed?"

"Marfa."

"Never been. Hear good things. Vaya con dios," he bids.

Puttering toward the car, I picture that guileless child shining brighter than the sun as she pedals down the block. Her biography was just beginning, and in the blink of an eye… it ended. And here's her grandfather, having laid her to rest. The pain and sorrow he's enduring must be harrowing. I'd bet my bottom dollar he'd swap places on the spot if conferred the opportunity.

"Mister!" he shouts, granting me a transitory reprieve from the fog inside my brain. "You can't imagine how much that meant to me." He lumbers back to the shrine, and I decamp, crestfallen.

REVOLUTIONARY ROAD

I'm cruising down a serene, four-lane motorway with five plus hours remaining when I bump into an unfamiliar noticeboard. The diamond-shaped placard indicates **WILDLIFE CROSSING**. Shit like this doesn't occur where I hang my hat. I decelerate, half-expecting coyotes, deer, and armadillos to prance across the asphalt – no dice.

Approaching Interstate 20 iconographic banners I'm convinced my designers photoshopped loll from the rafters of an outdoor concert venue promoting an upcoming performance by the incomparable Willie Nelson. In recognition of the luminary, I wail his classic "On the Road Again." It's a doggone shame I didn't bring a doobie and handle of rye to pay Shotgun Willie a fittin' tribute. A cig and Red Bull are forced to hack it.

Entering the Sweetwater municipality, I remark a tract of Himalayan wind turbines as far as the eye can see. It summons up the San Gorgonio Pass abutting Palm Springs, but that pales in comparison. This here is the **Roscoe Wind Farm**, formerly the largest in its category globally.

Leonardo DiCaprio and I believe it's pivotal to seek alternate techniques to produce power through renewable energy, instead of fossil fuels, in an attempt to protect the environment and possibly save the planet. Time out. I've got a confession to make. Those aren't my words. They merely replicate an ideology Leo would publicize. In addition, as king of the world, I'd wager it fosters his carnal exploits astronomically. Shagging that much trim sounds exhausting. Dude deserves a hiatus. I'm requesting posse membership, coupled with admission to the overflow. Post-induction, there's no doubt I'll alleviate a smidge of L.D.'s burden. It's an utterly charitable act.

Joking aside, I genuinely respect his environmental pursuits, and they were the catalyst behind augmenting my awareness. By harnessing the wind, these turbines create reliable, cost-effective, pollution-free energy, generating enough electricity in less than one hour to charge a household for an entire month. Each expands approximately four hundred feet, positioned three football fields apart. After the final group vanishes, I probe the odometer. Roughly twenty-five miles elapsed subsequent to the initiatory batch. What's weirdly engrossing – zee Germans own and operate this development. I can't resist tooting the horn in solidarity with those who manufactured the Benz as I hurtle into the wide blue yonder.

LOW & SLOW

Make no bones about it, I'm fixin' ta git to Marfa ASAFP, but my tummy's growling, dictating I consume a legit three-course meal. The more I daydream of food, the more I'm hankerin' for a bona fide Lone Star State cookout. I comb the map to expose Midland's **Up In Smoke BBQ Co.** is round the corner. As I redirect the GPS, my appetite lubricates. Sho'nuff, in two shakes of a lamb's tail, I'm queued near a crowded house, gorging themselves on abundant portions of edibles.

"What'll it be, darlin'?" the cashier inquires.

I browse the menu and decree, "The brisket and ribs plate."

"And which sides?"

"Potato salad and hatch mac & cheese. And a Shiner, assuming you stock it."

"Bless your heart," she says earnestly. On the contrary, her supercilious facial expression insinuates she deems me a damn fool. "$23.63, hon."

I fork over a triad of crisp Hamiltons and ponder telling her where she can stick the change, but you don't mess with Texas, and I ain't running the risk of a disgruntled Texan hocking a loogie in my chow.

"We'll call your number when it's ready," she instructs, surrendering the bottle of suds and a receipt that has lucky thirteen scrawled across the header.

The alfresco banquet area is beset with handcrafted picnic tables. As I'm poised to hunker down on a bench, my phone vibrates. I glug the brew and gag upon reading the notification. It's a text from Zoe.

Hey hotshot, she writes. *How's the trip?*

HI! So far so good. Practically there.

Outstanding. Just wanted to confirm everything was A-OK.

You worried about me?

Purely part of the customer service I provide to my clients, she stresses neighboring a *smirking face emoji*.

Does this imply I'm not unique?

You one of a kind

Yeah girl!

Cocky mofo

I type *LOL* then erase it. Grow up. I double tap and click *HAHA* then desist, devising a witty comeback. *Brace yourself for bad news… Crashed the car in a ditch.* The iMessage ellipsis pulses and I sweat her rebuttal.

LMAO Pity you waived the insurance.

FUCK!

A *smiling face with tear emoji* crystallizes alongside *Do me a favor. No tattling to my boss.*

Huh?

The texting. I'm violating the renter-rentee privilege.

They could disbar you, I sass. *Punishment by spanking at the very least.* Muzzle it, Casanova. *Don't panic. I'll keep your flirtatious antics safe. Snitches get stitches!*

She sends *TTYL* and the *face blowing a kiss emoji*, effectuating a Hallmark ending because…

"Number thirteen, your order is ready. Thirteen, order up," booms through the PA.

Commandeering the tray, I come to the realization my eyes are incontrovertibly bigger than my stomach – YOLO. I'm synchronously parking my keister and clawing at the entrée. The brisket melts in my mouth. It's sliced lean, and as succulent as can be. The charred bark dispatches yet another layer to this explosion of flavor. Holy mackerel I've seen too many episodes of *Diners, Drive-Ins and Dives* and morphed into Guy Fieri sans the atrocious hairstyle and hideous wardrobe. I devour the sliver, then flip-flop meats.

As expected, the pork is scrumptious. Undertones of pecan, black pepper, and mesquite mix palatably with the tangy glaze, and I'm summarily a whole rack deep, flesh slathered in sauce. I glom a towelette and sponge the marinade, then swill the bock lager. The cheesy macaroni follows, and it's a culinary sensation. I've long had a penchant for green chiles, and those of the hatch genus mesh the optimum ratio of sweet and heat to the creamy pasta dish. The potato salad doesn't compare. Stabbing at a pile of pickled onions and intermingling them enlivens the recipe. Shut the front door. That's out of bounds.

At this instance, I detect I'm being monitored. A nuclear family glares at me, and the patriarch contorts disdainfully. Apparently, I've been moaning with every bite – akin to Meg Ryan in *When Harry Met Sally*. I lower the utensil and cower from the Styrofoam.

"I'm awfully sorry," I tender to the terrified clan. Historically, my humiliation would stymie consummation, but curse proper etiquette. This feast is off the chain, and nobody knows me here. I plunge back into the brisket, snarfing it completely, then imbibe the Shiner. Dessert consists of a Parliament as I digest. Yee haw!

FURIOSA

The conclusive leg channels me down a desolate path. I'm zipping across the terrain at 85 mph, braking only as legally sanctioned when traveling the small rural towns in Pecos County. From afar I spy flames shooting out of a cannon-esque apparatus. At dusk, it evokes the Charlize Theron/Tom Hardy *Mad Max* reboot. A formidable complex manifesting the earmarks of an oil refinery blossoms. The expanse is too sizable to be definitive – not that it matters. I'm hypnotized by the resplendence.

My predilection for fire began circa 1995. Catherine Harrington lit a match on the playground, and we ogled the chemical reaction. Thereafter, Bunsen burners, pyrotechnics, stoves, and the like, have both intimidated and fascinated me. The primary alibi corroborating why I puff cigarettes is to assert dominance over an object of volatile combustion. I've oft stared at the tip and marveled at the veracity I'm holding something so potentially destructive between my fingers. Tee-hee. I snub the topography as I'm locked onto the rearview, watching the sparks flare until they dissolve into the shadows.

An eroded, bronzy carving in the outline of a mountain ingratiates commuters to Alpine, Texas. A potpourri of mom-and-pop shops and eateries delineate the downtown, evincing a homey ambiance. Converging upon the winking red, I surveil a swarm of choppers and a caliginous scrim fastened to the property on the northwest flank, introducing the **BIG BEND BIKER HOTEL** and **OLD GRINGO COFFEE & COCKTAILS**. It uncloaks a handlebar mustachioed, cowboy-hatted skeleton donning sunglasses. The illustration maintains a spooky similarity to ZZ Top's Billy Gibbons. Delayed at the light, I give careful deliberation to dropping in for libations and hobnobbing with the townies. I start visualizing how this movie scene might unfold.

FADE IN:

EXT. STREET - EVENING

A white MERCEDES BENZ draws up parallel to an assembly of HARLEY-DAVIDSONS. A middle-aged HIPSTER activates his security system via a KEY FOB, and a BEEP, BEEP chimes.

INT. OLD GRINGO'S BAR - MOMENTS LATER

The resident HELLS ANGELS, garbed in leather, huddle to inspect.

EXT. SIDEWALK

The hipster perambulates nonchalantly, then enters the BIG BEND BIKER HOTEL.

INT. BIG BEND BIKER HOTEL LOBBY

He wanders into the lobby, progressing toward the bar.

INT. OLD GRINGO'S BAR - MOMENTS LATER

"Tequila" by The Champs clatters from the jukebox.

The hipster trespasses, undaunted.

The record SCRATCHES, and as the tune
abruptly terminates, we reveal the
Hells Angels, gobsmacked. The LEADER
OF THE PACK jostles through his
subordinates. He scrutinizes the
hipster, stem to stern.

                    LEADER OF THE PACK
                  Get him!

The Hells Angels BUM-RUSH the hipster,
fists clenched, primed to brawl, and...

There's a honk at my six, and I resume along U.S. 67 inside
the stable confines of my CLA Coupe, homestretch in sight. Next
stop, Marfa.

TOP OF THE WORLD

As the speed limit decreases, I beam so jubilantly my cheeks ache. To the south, a multicolored billboard above log stanchions, planted in the vegetation reads **WELCOME TO MARFA ESTABLISHED 1883**. I have arrived!

I'm knackered, but a spontaneous flurry of eagerness weaves through my veins, coaxing me to gather intelligence. I creep at a snail's pace with my head on a swivel. Ostensibly, there isn't much pizzazz pending a gallery labeled **BALLROOM MARFA**. Music wafts out the postern while partygoers spill into the gloam. Nosing up to the traffic signal at the intersection of San Antonio and Highland, **The Hotel Paisano**'s behemoth, rooftop neon illuminates the dimmed avenue. The inoperative **HOWARD PETROLEUM** gas station publishes quirky fuel prices representing cannabis consumption and simultaneous oral stimulation. Silly, pot-toking, cunnilingus-crazed Marfans.

Farther down, **COCHINEAL**, purportedly the premier dining option and the exact place I've landed a rez at mañana. Dead ahead, the mandatory theological sanctuary – **St. Mary Catholic Church**. A statue of its namesake burgeons from a fantastic bed of rocks across the lawn. The district's quiet, and I infer that the nightlife here, synonymous with countless tourist traps, lessens significantly during the winter. Case in point, a bulletin stapled to **Planet Marfa** beer garden circulates **CLOSED FOR THE SEASON**. Since when is drinking seasonal? Wussies.

An oxidized lightboard incandesces **CAPRI** fronting an uber-hip warehouse constructed of smooth concrete and metal. The premises are segmented into two disparate experiences. On one end, revelers boozing at the modish cantina. Blasé foodies indulge on the other.

Transiting the thoroughfare, an emboldened font spelling **THUNDERBIRD** backlit in cerulean juts from iron rods strung over prickly pears. The refurbished motel ascends behind. Beyond that… nihility, subtracting a **Dairy Queen**. And although there's never an inopportune Blizzard juncture, I gotta hit the hay.

I bust a u-ey, and before you can say chocolate chip cookie dough, I'm at **HOTEL SAINT GEORGE**. I cut the motor and sit immobile as fatigue drenches me. Exiting the vehicle, I whine, "Oy vey!" unintentionally imitating somebody's bubbe and nearly crumple. My muscles have fully stiffened, and they're revolting with tremendous cause. I should practice yoga or jazzercise. A few basic calisthenics will do the trick temporarily. Seconds after, I'm as good as… well, poop, quite frankly. Unlocking the trunk slopes my cerebral Panavision Tarantino-style. Atypical of QT, travel equipment supplants the cadavers and weaponry. I clutch the backpack and disco indoors like a gimpy Vincent Vega.

A fetching damsel – sandy brown curls, amiable demeanor, obligatory greeter twinkle – embraces me. In lieu of a standard uniform, she's sporting a charcoal denim shirt and onyx jeans. Copycat.

"Howdy, sir."

"Shalom. Checking in," I reply, handing her my ID.

"Splendid," she communicates, thwacking the keyboard. "Ah, welcome back."

I glower disapprovingly. "Nope, newbie."

Her forehead wrinkles, contemplation heightens from the screen. "Hmm, my mistake, I guess," she apologizes unapologetically. "Two nights in a deluxe king?"

"Yes, ma'am."

"Groovy. Swipe your card for incidentals, and we're all set." As I comply, she skids a branded key holder across the desk. "You're on the third floor, room 313. The elevator bank is behind this divider. Breakfast begins at 7:30 a.m. and finishes at 11 a.m. Lunch service ensues til 2 p.m. Happy hour runs 4 to 6 p.m., and our restaurant opens at 5:00 p.m. Dinner suspends by 10 p.m., and the bartenders generally evict everyone round midnight. Questions linked to the hotel or town overall, don't hesitate to dial zero on the landline. Anything else I may assist with?"

"Your name," I implore, testing the waters mischievously.

"Ariel," she familiarizes invitingly, exuding what's certifiably false hope that there's a fighting chance at coercing her into a schtickle of consensual, nocturnal hedonism in the short term.

"Pretty name for a pretty girl. And you've been most helpful. I'm going upstairs to hibernate."

"Enjoy your stay," she proffers, unveiling a provocative grin.

I do a double take, influencing her to chuckle. Ariel, you naughty little mermaid you. Let a fella snooze first, sheesh. I make myself scarce while still harboring the willpower.

DISTINCTLY MARFA

I affix the privacy tag on the outer handle, then slouch against the door, drained. A casual glance validates my selection. Snazzy setup, as promised. Rest assured, I'll find oodles to complain about later. Presently, I require sleep. Pre-sleep, I require soap. I'm repellent.

I hurl my gear onto the ottoman and assail the bathroom. Rotating the shower lever, I'm taken aback by a kooky, wooden stool plopped in the corner. It echoes a tree stump. How many nude asses have straddled… this… thing? Blech. I gawk inquisitively, cogitating whether to uproot it. I'll ask housekeeping to do the grunt work.

I calibrate the electric toothbrush to overdrive and spend an inordinate stint expunging a pack's worth of toxic residue. My reflection dwindles as steam billows, until a heavy mist obscures the mirror. I strip my outfit and step inside, where I'm promptly reminded of the gratification reaped from a piping hot cleanse after an arduous odyssey. I pamper myself like *Parks and Recreation*'s Tom and Donna on "Treat Yo' Self Day", emptying the brunt of the Aēsop formulations in one fell swoop.

With the grime of the road rinsed free, I tie a towel around my midriff and wipe the condensation off the glass. Ridding enough moisture to unshroud my profile, I fall into a trance. Depletion notwithstanding, I'm engulfed by a true sense of victory. Mission accomplished. Finally made it to Marfa. And having journeyed an uninterrupted twenty some-odd hours, I ain't gonna lie… your boy's a hunk… if you omit that pesky scar beneath my right eye. It's relatively inconspicuous unless you're really searching, but I abhor that blemish. What bugs me most is I can't dredge up how it resulted. Perhaps from an excessive quaffing of Irish Car Bombs amidst a fateful St. Paddy's celebration. I blacked out and regained consciousness at the bottom of a staircase. That's solely conjecture. I vaguely recall seeing it, then being unable to unsee it ever again.

Darby contends it adds character. I presumed she was just trying to be cordial. People do that shit. When they insist, "you can hardly tell," it intimates they're flat-out lying. And I'd know because I coined that line. Personally, I viewed the scar as yet another imperfection added to a mounting list of faults. At any rate, the ladies never cared, and I've learned to cope. So it goes.

I cease self-deprecating, clothe in a tee and boxers, then switch my mobile to 'leave me the hell alone' mode. Why's the room sweltering? Dear lord! Some maniac adjusted the thermostat to a balmy seventy-seven degrees. A comrade once told me Bill Gates regulates his fortress at seventy-two, and thus, I must follow suit. Spinning gracefully, I jack my arms, salute the invisible judges, then springboard atop the comforter with such flawlessness I eclipse Greg Louganis for the gold medal. I crawl under the covers blissful as my vacation has officially begun.

REBEL WITHOUT A KAWS

The unremitting whistle of a rumbling freighter rouses me from my slumber as I stretch my joints with a yawn. Clock blazons 6:23 a.m., meaning that for the first time in recent memory, I've gotten more than ten hours of shut-eye. Hallelujah.

I retract the drapery, and Nina Simone immerses me. A full day of sights awaits. I enrobe in joggers, trainers, a hoodie, and lightweight parka. Almost ready. Fervently, I unpack my Tom Ford Ribbed Cashmere beanie and Tom Ford Snowdon shades. How else can I ensure I'm Marfa's supremo fashionista? I seize the Polaroid, a film packet, an envelope, and Sharpie, then bounce.

Brekkie isn't served this early, so I pay a visit to **MARFA BURRITOS** just a hop, skip, and a jump away. A Latina woman preps ingredients in the kitchen, and I decide now is the ideal circumstance to utilize my amateur Spanish vocabulary.

"Buenos dias. Cómo estás?"

"Muy bien."

"Un chorizo y huevos con queso por favor." Check out the big brain on me! I'm a smart motherfucker.

She nods, then rattles off a paragraph of español in rapid-fire succession. I goggle absently. Sensing my inability to comprehend the words coming from her mouth, she chirps, "Two minutes," making me appear an even greater dunce.

Deflated, I reverse and gaze around the room at the walls of fame. Well, I'll be a monkey's uncle. Anthony Bourdain, Mark Ruffalo, and Matthew McConaughey ate here? Alright, alright, alright.

"Siete dólares, señor," the disparaging biddy articulates. I pony up a tenner, instructing her to keep the change… in English. "Gracias, guapo," she responds with unfeigned gratitude.

"De nada, señorita," I reply, and I'm back in business, baybee!

Proceeding west along San Antonio pilots me toward the previous evening's sneak peek. The moment I surpass DQ, it's uncharted territory, and I heed my locale closely. The **BUNS N' ROSES** café faces the **CEMENTERIO DE LA MERCED** burial ground. I'm iffy about situating a diner opposite a field of death. On one hand, nothing says funeral like a hearty meal post-casket drop, and voilà. On the other hand, ghosts. But what do I know? And registering that the lot's inundated with customers suggests Axl, Slash, and Duff are astute restauranteurs, and I should zip my lip.

Just up the way, a severely corroded, retro motel sign protrudes from the thicket. **S-T-A-R-D-U-S-T** descends one letter below the next. As dawn emerges, it's easy to construe the word **MARFA** has ousted MOTEL. There's a curious allure to this weathered piece of West Texas lore, representative of the last vestiges of old Vegas. Those vibrant displays that helped make Sin City fabulous during its heyday only to get thrown on the scrapheap in the Neon Boneyard.

Six miles forward I behold... uh, er... a mammoth cardboard cutout of... a human? I'm stupefied. Drawing closer, complementary figures materialize. I pull onto the gravelly verge and recce. Illogically, someone erected a towering *Giant* mural in this otherwise barren patch. A fifteen-foot-tall James Byron Dean dons an unbuttoned, jade polo with a rifle slung across his shoulders. He's bookended by the voluptuous Elizabeth Taylor, leaning against a pillar, and the ruggedly handsome Rock Hudson, tenanting a lemon convertible. At their backs, George Stevens lounges on his director's chair, overlooking a replica of the movie's mansion.

As though the exhibit isn't adequately baffling, I hear a melody emanating. A weakly fabricated, barbed wire fencing is the lone deterrent from investigating further. Dreading hidden claymore mines putting my expedition in jeopardy prevents it. Alternatively, I squat to diagnose and ferret out weeds concealing two proportional granite lumps, the contours of speaker grills built squarely onto the mineral. That's bizarre. I had no clue such a gadget existed, and I'm left questioning if the inventor of this crackpot doohickey also pioneered the tree stump shower stool. I trigger the Shazam app on my iPhone. It quickly identifies the ditty as "Release" by The Monkees' Michael Nesmith. The connotation eludes me. I philosophize the curator couldn't secure the rights to John, Paul, George, or even Ringo and settled for the Yankee Doodle knockoff.

Dusting the smut as I straighten, I spot a ranch gate pronouncing **LITTLE REATA** – the manor Jimmy's Jett Rink persona controlled. Not far off, the actual, dilapidated prop he scaled to recon his newly inherited plot upon which he'd strike oil. I'm astonished these remained intact for sixty-five years.

I nick the camera and snap a photo of the plywood actors. It slides into my palm, and I abstain from shaking the negative back and forth, no matter how badly I want to. Sorry, Outkast – blame my therapist. While it develops, I nab photos of the artifacts. After they've processed entirely, I write the month, day, and year on the borders, unclasp the glove compartment, and wedge them within the envelope for safekeeping.

Prior to persevering, I absorb this most prodigious backdrop. Everything seems infinite here. Conjure a mental picture of a spellbinding Jacob van Ruisdael landscape or the establishing shot of an epic cinematic western. Ethereal cloud scuds drift through the stratosphere. Farm animals forage the verdant meadow. The grandiose Davis Mountains sit amongst the sweeping hills. It's a sensory overload.

Having accepted I can't subsist without the distractions of metropolitan living, this trip has shown me all that I take for granted. There is so much beauty in the world. Regrettably, I seldom slow down to appreciate it. Yet as I gape at the heavens, I am preoccupied by the voice of my father looming inside my ever-wandering mind.

"Red sky at night, sailors' delight. Red sky in morning, sailors warning," he recited to me when I was a lad. In layman's terms, it forebodes if the sun sets in a pinkish tint, tomorrow will be at your fingertips. On the flip side, there's a contingency things may get turbulent if resurrecting to an analogous milieu. At present, a delicate rouge fuses with the azure, and I'm praying dad's aphorism doesn't come to fruition.

MAC AND ME AND PABLO

I'm Marty McFlyin' at 88 mph. There's zilch perceptible discounting the countryside. The King Kong-sized pop art diverted me from my vittles, and I'm hangry as all get-out. I dip into the paper bag and inhale that delectable aroma. Let's go! With knees guiding the wheel, I peel back the parchment and sink my teeth in. Chewing the cheesy egg and sausage amalgamation is titillating, and I squeal lasciviously. Wow! I need a girlfriend. Evidently, I substitute food for intimacy. Maybe because the food doesn't bicker and it's whoppingly more affordable. Additionally, no female has supplied unrestrained pleasure to the breadth food does. Even Devin, and she was obscenely attentive.

On the brink of chomp número dos, I twig a peculiar image overhead. Some sort of aircraft moves languidly. A helicopter? A puddle jumper? The fuselage mimics a compact Goodyear Blimp. I lose track of the shuttle in the murk until it skirrs through, inflating exponentially. I'm mystified and growing increasingly freaked every second. Anxiety surging from the pit of my stomach.

I gun the engine attempting to outrun the damn thing. My grapple on the tortilla loosens, and it tumbles onto the mat. I'm not one to believe in the supernatural but haven't been given any reason to either. I can't stop shivering, and before I know what's happening, I'm careening along U.S. 90 West, topping 100 mph, with the extraterrestrial spacecraft closing fast.

There's an indecipherable placard ahead and a byway behind. Turn or keep moving? The UFO stays hot on my tail, and although my initial instinct is to flee, something inwardly screams, "seek refuge!" As the drive nears, I swerve across the dotted yellows. SHIT! I slam the brakes, and my bumper comes to a halt inches from the gated entrance. Fear-induced insanity saturates my arteries. I leap out of the car and stampede toward the barricade, optics aimed at a humongous circular landing strip below. My vigilance fluctuates to the panel's messaging –

Tethered Aerostat Radar System U.S. Customs and Border Protection. Blisteringly, I oscillate between the verbiage, the tarmac, and the vessel, ad nauseam.

My head droops, vanquishing the consternation. Unadulterated laughter bellows into the zephyr. I'm guffawing madly, characteristic of a lunatic. I'll never admit confessing this, and if you gossip, I'll gouge out your spleen. I'm an absolute dumbass.

Anybody owning a Netflix subscription in the 2010s likely underwent a massive *Narcos* phase, same as me. My obsession grew so huge that I gobbled up all I could relating to the cocaine trade. Amid said period, I pondered quitting music and transforming into the Midwestern Escobar – that's neither here nor there. This cosmic Hindenburg is actually a low-level airborne surveillance mechanism employed to derail drug traffickers from penetrating American airspace undetected. I knew these resided in Arizona, New Mexico, and Florida, but wasn't aware Marfa had become a hotbed for narcotics smuggling. The United States Office of Homeland Security obviously rendered it prudent to implement a TARS precinct which computes insofar as we're sixty miles north of the Mexican border.

The concept of getting blown to smithereens by E.T.'s murderous cousins has dissipated, and now I'm romanticizing about snorting lines of yayo. Owing to the fact it's barely daybreak and I don't possess any nose candy, I reach a compromise with myself. I reconstruct the dismantled breakfast burrito, scarfing it down lickety-split. **Mental note:** ask the hotel concierge to furnish contact info for a regional drug dealer.

1837 MILES WEST

A speed monitoring trailer flashes at me to slacken to 35 mph, infiltrating the town of Valentine, population 217. Idling through the decay, I'm stricken with sadness. It mirrors a location from Denzel Washington's *The Book of Eli*. An apocalyptic state of destruction: ramshackle structures revealing shattered windows, roofs torn off, veneers ripped to shreds. Just past the assumably defunct **Sacred Heart Catholic Church**, the **Valentine Veterans Memorial** crops up, prompting me to wonder if all bygone inhabitants met their maker at the unspecified battle this monument commemorates.

However, a mile and a half beyond that hurly-burly stands **PRADA MARFA**. Fortuitously, I'm the sole individual here. I park and frolic over, giddy. It's doubly spectacular in person. At first sight, it legitimately passes for a true-blue storefront. This might be a mirage. I grope the sun-dried clay exterior to authenticate I'm not trippin' tits. It's conceivable the burrito wench slipped me a Mickey, and considering my brush with intergalactic warfare, I demand guarantees. Sure enough, the installation is the real McCoy.

A rusted fence wraps around the perimeter, prominently dangling a smorgasbord of padlocks. I witnessed a congruent exposition when my then college steady and I went to Paris. They're classified as love locks, attached by transient couples proclaiming their mutual affection. The Pont des Arts bridge was similarly decorated, and we resolved to pledge our devotion via participating in the ritual. Upon our return, I dumped the skank after she cheated with her French professor. Oh, the irony. It's like rain on your wedding day. Many moons ago, I flew back to Gay Paree for Lollapalooza, resolute about removing that wretched padlock. Before resorting to the acquisition of bolt cutters, I'd been informed the gendarme had them excised in 2015.

Pageantry such as this has endured for decades throughout Europe. Shockingly, the trend found its way to Far West Texas. Kinda makes me wanna reconnect with the broad. I heard she got divorced and gained a ton of weight. I'd derive sadistic enjoyment strutting my accomplishments and polished physique. Bitter? Moi?

I retrace my steps to peruse the inventory. Three tiers of shelves tout women's heels – a mishmash of types and tones. The showroom parades black and pink purses aloft lacquered bases in diverging alignments. Rectangular merchant banners garnish both sides of the sealed door. The awnings below advertise the proprietary emblem. I toddle to the fringe and soak it up. It's fascinating. I cannot fathom the menagerie of hallucinogens Elmgreen and Dragset consumed that sparked the idea.

I haul out my cell and photograph the whole enchilada: the edifice, the couture, the steel treachery. As a bonus, I mug for a few selfies, then reacquire the Polaroid. I capture a wide shot of the configuration, scribble the date, and insert it into the pouch. Basking in the glory, I scorch a cigarette and scroll the roll.

Social media ruined civilization, but you're nobody unless somebody sees your post and likes it. Even so, I don't maintain Facebook or Twitter accounts anymore. I'd grown sick and tired of users' daily rants and motivational quotations. And, well, TikTok addicts are imbeciles. Nevertheless, I get a kick out of Instagram for the pure 'look at what I'm doing this instant' aspect. Plus, I adore pictures, and I'm vain as fuck. I upload my fave, stamp the filter, and away I go.

GOOD TO THE LAST DROP

Vrooming back toward the hotel, I uncover the TARS fettered to the runway. What had earlier led to frenzy and anguish elicits a titter — it emulates a cartoon rocket ship. I envision loafing alongside Marvin the Martian, ALF, and the cast of *Rick and Morty*, hoovering preposterous quantities of blow. My parents would be super proud.

Farther east I cross paths with a carbon copy of the WELCOME TO MARFA billboard I saw yesterday. Since I didn't snag a photo then… I climb out, smack-dab in the center of the lane, and shoot.

I've got time to kill, thereby opting to off-load the rental and take a leisurely stroll around the downtown. I happen upon a coffee shop named **THE SENTINEL** and conclude a mid-morning pick-me-up involving Colombia's second finest export is consequential.

"What sounds promising?" the barista asks gaily.

"Lavender latte with oat milk and Splenda, please," I solicit, feeling ultra-vanilla.

"Excellent choice," he declares in the manner of a snobby maître d' at a Michelin-starred eatery, complimenting a patron who orders a bottle of '96 Château Lafite Rothschild. I wink in acknowledgment of my imperial request and plunk a buck into his tip jar.

The room effuses a dapper, avant-garde vibe, combining southern rustic with Restoration Hardware posh. Equipale barrel chairs, cowhide rugs, sling hammocks, and reclaimed wood tables embellish the spacious interior. The masonry melds exposed brick with neatly chiseled plaster. Legions of floating mantels stage miniature cacti, pottery, and baskets. The playlist blends old-school DJ Shadow with new-school SG Lewis.

I flop down next to a Mr. and Mrs. bedecked in heinous Bohemian chic, waxing poetic about spirituality. Their chocolate Labrador lies atop the laminate, bored shitless. He regards me with those sad puppy dog eyes, yearning to be rescued. Eavesdropping on the discussion has me sympathetic to his plight. I shift concentration elsewhere before the retriever cons me into aiding and abetting his liberation.

I begin leafing through a magazine and come across an editorial concerning the top ten eras of art. As I anticipate scoping the scene later this afternoon, I figure why not. Besides, I've checked my DMs and could use a respite from responding to my idiotic followers inquiring what I copped at the Prada store.

Whereas I'm an advocate for the arts, by and large, I'm also the first to concede the ABCs are Greek to me. I've perennially accumulated urban graffiti screen prints, concert posters, and revered litho reproductions, which I misrepresent as the genuine article. Trust me, my cronies are none the wiser. I gravitate toward items that hold a special place or kindle emotions. I have no desire to bone up on its history and probably won't unless I'm bone-ing a student majoring in the subject. See what I did there?

Lichtenstein, Basquiat, Magritte – that's my jam. But David Hockney is the G.O.A.T. His collage titled Pearblossom Hwy., 11-18 April 1986, #2 piqued my interest in the topic and contributed plenty with revitalizing my passion for road trips. Our introductory meeting occurred during a sojourn in the City of Angels. I attended an industry conference and snuck away from the monotonous seminars to tour The Getty. As I strode the halls, appraising the respective bodies of work, Hockney's stood head and shoulders above. It features upwards of seven hundred overlapping stills, photographed at varying angles along the notorious Route 138 in the Antelope Valley.

The montage demonstrates the conflicting perspectives inside an automobile. The driver's viewpoint, depicted on the right, emphasizes the objects descried whilst at the controls – signposts and pavement markings, for example. The left signifies that of the passenger, and though highly detailed, notably less important to safety – discarded soda cans, beer bottles, a motor oil canister, and supplementary refuse litter the scrub in the forefront of a clump of Joshua trees surfacing from the Mojave undergrowth. It conveys the impression of two travelers on a vehicular voyage encapsulated within a singular graphic.

What's most compelling is how Hockney conflates Cubist notions of space and realism. I'm screwing with you. I'd beat my own ass for saying that balderdash aloud. My unrefined palate simply thinks Pearblossom Highway is dope.

The java artisan delivers the cup and rushes off. I snare it and sip. Goddamn! That's a tasty beverage. It's not cocaine good, but it's pretty fucking good. I fling the periodical and amble back to the counter.

"Everything satisfactory?" he frets.

"Positively sublime."

"Terrific."

"Do you, perchance, have any dog treats?"

"Coincidentally," he pauses and extracts a tin, "we're endorsing these nutritious, dehydrated, grass-fed beef bites. They're humane, sustainable, and locally sourced."

"Mmmm, yummy," I retort sarcastically. The dingbat dispenses a sprinkling of kibble. It looks like cat poo as opposed to a morsel for man's best friend. Betcha they're vegan. God, I hate vegans. I meander toward the pooch and crouch to feed him. "Hang in there, bud," I encourage. His egocentric masters fail to notice. He licks my fingers, and I reciprocate with an ear rub, then bound for the sidewalk.

EVERYTHING IN ITS WRONG PLACE

Lots of folks leg it when inspecting the highlights of Marfa. Chumps. Us foresighted strategists charter electric bicycles. I promenade down Abbot, curve east onto San Antonio and I'm at **ebikemarfa**. They've assigned me a RadRover Fat-tire to tool around on. This bad mama jama can travel forty-five miles per charge. Bearing in mind the town's total area measures under two square miles denotes I won't exert that much energy.

The soundtrack for today's adventure is Radiohead. Songs composed by Thom Yorke, Jonny Greenwood, and the lads exemplify the crème de la crème of experimental rock. I commence with my personal darling, "Talk Show Host." Distributed as a B-side, this mere afterthought attained a rebirth once licensed for Baz Luhrmann's *Romeo + Juliet*. In my humble opinion, it bridged the gap between the subtle splendor of *The Bends* and the groundbreaking innovation of *OK Computer*. I press the polygon and pedal off on my one-man exploration.

In theory, Marfa's housing market is completely out of whack. The median income hovers near $42,000. Meanwhile, the average price for available residences exceeds $400,000. This due partly to the real estate speculators and affluent vacationers scooping up every property they could get their grubby paws on.

Gliding hither and thither, I review numerous adobes, mid-century moderns, and stuccos, struggling to withstand the test of time. In sharp contrast, they're surrounded by an exorbitance of teardowns, jaw-dropping rehabs from well-renowned architects, and tiny homes vaunting cutesy nicknames. The ritzier abodes merge glass, concrete, and corrugated metals. They dub it high-desert style, which basically implies cosmopolitan wealth… in the desert.

For as many *Wallpaper**-worthy domiciles I've scouted, there's practically as many doublewides and shanties. A generous fragment of the substandard living nests southward and canvassing those neighborhoods unfurls a garish billboard accentuating a random owl hooting that **EL COSMICO** dwells over yonder. Spying inside brandishes heaps of glamping shelters. I chortle mockingly at the adjoining outhouse. A tilting of my noodle positions me in the trajectory of the **McGuire Ranch**, where PTA filmed *There Will Be Blood*. Hard pass. Method actors are cuckoo for Cocoa Puffs. I'm afraid Danny Boy lurks in the wings, itching to Bill the Butcher me.

Wheeling away, I stumble upon **COBRA ROCK** and brake impulsively, skidding to a stop. Peering through the pane at a sampling of handmade boots, I'll attest I'm rubbernecking a skosh too lustfully, but the fastidious craftsmanship is stellar! It's imperative I score a pair toot sweet. Torturously, on the back burner it goes. In the context of auditioning garments and consummating momentous wardrobe decisions, I'm a diva. Empirical evidence supports this activity requiring hours. Therefore, like the Terminator...

Throttling north, I arrive at an honest-to-goodness, coin-operated payphone fronting The Lincoln Marfa and contemplate calling someone collect for shits and giggles. Lifting the handset, I discover that an unidentified deviant has rigged the contraption to transmit Taylor Swift's "Shake It Off" and it blasts into my eardrum. Son of a bitch! That's a nasty trick... yet I listen all the way because I'm a closet Swifty.

Within close range, flags symbolizing Texas and the U.S.A. flutter outside the **Presidio County Courthouse**. Lady Justice rises atop the middle dome, hemmed by stunning Roman arches. Diagonal to the municipal building, a vertical, emerald marquee intersects an art deco shell. They've converted the erstwhile **PALACE** movie theater into an illustrator's studio, but the original overlay and canopy perdure.

In the background, stationed betwixt them, an imposing, silvery water tower looms. This isn't any old water tower. *This* is the iconic **Marfa Water Tower**, and it's unequaled. The shimmering radiance spawns the appearance of a pewter sculpture rather than a functional holding tank. From such vantage point, I'm able to obtain Polaroids of three of the town's most noteworthy landmarks.

Coasting along Highland, I confront a strip of charming boutiques. The bellwether – **ESPERANZA VINTAGE**, predominantly catering to dames boasting impeccable taste in premium clothing. I'm cognizant of this thanks to Darby. There's a litany of beguiling, handwoven, Native American coats pinned onto the Sheetrock. My BFF stipulated I'd bestow a "Chimayo" upon her as a reward for house-sitting. Drawn from the pics she forwarded me I deduce these are commensurate. Glimpsing the tag, I jeer at the requisition. I'm confident the $600 is warranted. I'm more confident she's left my cupboards bare, not to mention the cost I'll incur dry-cleaning the linens. She'll have to make do with an inexpensive tchotchke.

I crank toward a hulking, stark white complex occupying an entire block. The surname **JUDD**, belonging to Donald Clarence Judd, stenciled above the doorsill. He's the exalted creative who came here almost fifty years prior and reputedly brought culture to a humdrum West Texas colony. I'm astounded at the synchronicity, as I was on the cusp of jettisoning the bike and driving to the museum that the Don Dada of Marfa launched. It must've been preordained.

ARTSY-FARTSY

A uniquely ostentatious assemblage of phrases ornamenting a timbered signboard directs me toward the parking lot. It's an unmitigated disaster of immensurable proportions. English and Spanish text erratically arrayed within a chunky tetragon, bilingually translating to the nomenclature of the museum – **THE CHINATI FOUNDATION**. Radical.

Hopping from the Benz, I survey multiple groupings of ginormous mortar slabs encrusting the campus. They're markedly consistent lock, stock, and barrel. Imagine a stupendously bland Stonehenge or materials at a construction site. Yo no comprendo. Suffice it to say, I bypass the in-depth examination and beeline for the lobby.

A Gen Z tandem clad in matching tees emblazoning the institution designation muck about on their laptops.

"Konnichiwa, y'all."

"May I help you?" the catatonic chap extends drably.

I skim the printed list of attendees and gesture at my name. "11:00 reservation."

"Superb, I'll check you in," the lass interjects, clicking the mouse. "You're good to go. Head through those doors, and your docent will join shortly."

"Ahem," the dullard incites, then becomes hushed.

"Speak."

"We have a strict no photo policy," he lectures lethargically, digit targeted at the camera. "Two options: consign that to us or return it to your vehicle."

"Huh?! The moose out front didn't tell me that."

"There's a moose out front?"

"There is?"

"I'm, er, I don't, uh…" the protocol Nazi stammers, unqualified to interpret my farcical citation nor manipulation tactics.

"Let me get this straight. Twenty bucks and zero photos?" I prod, aggravated.

"Yes," the nymph replies abjectly. "The founders believed it detracted from a true engagement with the art."

"What if I just grab a quickie using my phone?"

"You'll be asked to leave," the pretentious little twit cautions pretentiously.

"Suppose I'll deposit this in the car then. Wouldn't wanna upset Naomi, Wynonna, or Ashley."

"Cheers. Enjoy the tour," he gibes demeaningly.

Hmm, this sure got off on the wrong foot. I retreat to the Mercedes, stewing, sacrifice the Polaroid, then corral a bottle of H2O. Certainly, they permit agua. We're in the boondocks for Chrissake.

I reenter the lobby and espy the fun police unsuccessfully explaining to a stereotypically touristy Asian couple why their froufrou Leicas are banned. Snickering, I waltz past to browse the merchandise. There's an oversized hardcover immortalizing the punter at the helm of this operation, and I read the inner flap.

According to the author, Donald Judd abides amongst the twentieth century's chief artistes. He rejected traditional methodology, instead choosing to dabble in the realm of three-dimensional space. It chronicles his Empire State triumphs and nascent Marfa transference, whereupon he accrued a significant percentage of the town. Then, with the benefaction of some multimillion-dollar, nonprofit organization, procured an extraneous 340 acres, including a decommissioned military base Chinati labels home. And lastly, it indicates he expired. So, provided I'm understanding this correctly, hombre was a lackluster painter, reinvented himself by employing an easier medium, became rich and famous, then transitioned into a land baron. Unfortunate he's pushing up daisies. Could've preempted Tony Robbins as the ultimate infomercial swami.

"Welcome to Chinati. I'm your docent, Jilly," the loony on the terrace acquaints. Her costume entailing horn-rimmed spectacles, Birkenstocks, and a safari hat, unkempt grey hair tucked underneath. The pièce de résistance – the buckled chin strap. "Today's tour inaugurates with Donald Judd's *100 untitled works in mill aluminum.* From there, we'll tackle Dan Flavin's seminal approach to fluorescents. And to top it off, a showing of John Chamberlain's esoteric sculptures.

"We're hiking roughly a mile and a quarter; thus, water is permissible, but eating and filming are prohibited, as well as bags and purses. Kindly stow them with our interns."

The regiment marches toward the first of two monstrous artillery sheds enveloping Judd's offerings. It's a remarkable specimen of engineering, twenty-five yards lengthwise or thereabouts. Dozens of capacious windows girdle the bricked façade, enabling ungodly amounts of natural light to flood in. The roofing parallels a bisected grain silo plonked onto the framework. I bulge with optimism and assume beyond the unaccommodating check-in twins, the arbitrary rules, and our eccentric jungle Sherpa, this excursion might not be too lousy when all is said and done. And then we pierce the aperture, and my joyful outlook fleetly wanes.

I maneuver row to row, analyzing the crates. Something's amiss. Each seems feckly identical: identical size, identical shape, identical plating. Microscopic variations prevail, yet mainly it's equivalent to staring at what a Xerox machine that spits out titanic platinum photocopies would produce. I feel like I'm taking crazy pills or trapped inside an episode of *The Twilight Zone.* I shut my eyelids, hoping to awaken from this puzzling incubus. Close, but no cigar.

I audit the spectators to gauge their reactions, anxious to unmask at least one congenial mortal. These charlatans are lapping up this poppycock. A bride and groom stand arm in arm, gawking at a bin as if it's the most fantabulous creation they've ever beheld.

Others caress the casing. That's definitely illegal. Another fraternity of sheeple huddle in deeply elitist conversation with relevance to how minimalism dethroned abstract expressionism as the au courant movement in the sixties. Jilly pantomimes wildly, while a quintet of aging women hangs on her every word. The dynamic Asian duo poses for a selfie. Euthanize me.

"Let's keep this train rollin' and progress to the second shed," she governs rhapsodically with the scrum in convoy.

It doesn't take long to peg these doodads appear interchangeable. The uniformity imbues my occipital lobe, and I shout, "Groundhog Day!" Everyone pivots and leers. I smirk uncomfortably as the humorless jagoffs scatter like mice. Ignoring them, I stalk each aisle, befogged. Clearly, the joke's on me. I wish they'd clue me in though. Enough already.

The phrase "art is subjective" crosses my mind. I've routinely deemed that utter bullshit, but never more so than right here, right now. Whatever these things are, art they are not. One thing I cannot dispute – ol' fuddy-juddy was an evil genius. He made a career of manufacturing these indistinguishable, chromium cubes, masquerading them as design, and getting compensated handsomely in the process. Don't hate the player, hate the game. Donny's the P. Diddy of the contemporary art world and has duped us, hook, line, and sinker. Bravo, sir, bravo.

I wander outdoors, sucking on a cig, as the sycophants venerate the Reynolds Wrap. I suspect smoking isn't permitted either. They can derelicte my balls. Soon after, the pack exits, following the leader west.

"Next up, Dan Flavin's *untitled*," Jilly educates. "Within these former army barracks, Flavin exhibits his bedazzling fixtures. During this segment of the tour, you're empowered to investigate at your own pace. You'll enter, trek down the passage, observe the arrangement, then turnabout, crisscross the quadrangle, and repeat.

There are six units altogether. I must remind you we've outlawed visual media. Resist the temptation to use your cell. Please keep it in your pants." I bite my tongue, refraining from pontificating on the docent's sexual innuendo.

They converge upon the barrack, and I slurp my liquid, then advance into the hollow darkness. I'm straining to see ahead as the throng impedes my visibility. Albeit inarguably frustrated, I play it cool, equipping these phonies with an ample spell to ogle. Piecemeal, they funnel out. Once the majority have vacated, I encroach.

The wattage exuded is pervasive, and I shield my peepers. Squinching at my hand, I'm smacked by the likelihood one of these assholes dosed me. I peek toward the water bottle. I peek toward the corners of the room. Back to the water bottle. Back to the corners of the room. I prophesize camouflaged amps will pound Swedish House Mafia. Eight elongated tubes, slanting left to right, expand floor to ceiling. The bulbs radiate green with a fuchsia hue glistening from behind.

I race out, perambulating the grassy midpoint, and troop through the remote module. These bulbs slant inversely, luminescing pink with a posterior clover glow. Am I being punked? I scamper to the succeeding unit. Two batches of ten entrenched side by side – half green, half pink. I hump to the other end, and unsurprisingly, it's the antonym of the latter. Nostradamus what's transpiring in barracks three and four. Same, same but different punctuating yellows and blues. Vertigo blooms, and currently I'm miffed my Dasani wasn't laced with MDMA. DJ Dan Flavin should headline the Sahara Tent at Coachella in favor of installing lightbulbs at a gallery. I've got a sneaking suspicion Judd acted as the Obi-Wan to his Skywalker.

The teachings of my father dictate to finish what you start, hence, like Kevin Costner I go the distance and vet the final layouts posthaste.

They're nominally stimulating, comprising all the colors, but I've been there, done that. Time to Houdini outta here. With punim lowered to avoid physical interaction, I tread explosively, fluidly, stoutly, robustly along the pathway. Docent Jilly clocks me and tailgates.

"*Sir, sir…*" she yells.

"No hablo inglés."

"*Sir, sir…*" she yells louder.

Begrudgingly, I revolve to brave her. "Yeah?!"

"There's still a component of the tour remaining. And if you thought Judd and Flavin were class, wait till ya get a load of Chamberlain," she gushes exultingly.

"The anticipation is killing me!" I exclaim sardonically. "Just gonna watch some paint dry, have a root canal, and give myself an enema. Apprise Wilt that I'll be there in a jiffy," I condescend, projecting a thumbs up. The docent manifests a quizzical lour. Before she can respond, I flip my mitt. Her eyebrows narrow. I bloat my cheeks and discharge a flatulence noise as an ode to *Happy Gilmore*. She jumps backward, perplexity running rampant. I whip out my iPhone and snap her picture. "Toodles!" I razz theatrically and gallop away. I finally realize why they won't sanction photography. If anyone saw this quote, unquote art preliminary to paying this hoax would file for Chapter 11. **Mental note:** I need a fucking drink!

HOLY TOLEDO

Since I haven't had my full James Dean fix, I hoof it to the Paisano, where the matinee idol previously boarded. Amid the jaunt from my hotel, I delve into the archives. Wikipedia claims that Henry C. Trost built this in 1930. Just so happens, Herr Trost is a fellow Mud Hen. Katie Holmes, Jamie Farr, Eric Kripke, and I are extremely gratified.

The patio centers around an opulent, tiered, Mediterranean fountain, characterizing the textbook definition of placidity. Sophistication personified faithfully describes the foyer, flaunting a marriage between Old Hollywood and West Texas. Genteel leather sofas and chairs swathe the lavish Spanish tile. Antique lamps and chandeliers establish the mood with a subdued luster. I'm digging the vibe until I scrutinize the jumbo heads of a bull and a buffalo mounted to the walls and extemporaneously squall, "Shit! Fuck!" Guests, minding their beeswax, scrap their endeavors to assess the Tourette's freak, and I'm impelled to beg forgiveness.

I've never understood taxidermy. Why anybody wants to possess a deceased anything boggles me. Hunters constitute the core enthusiasts, and despite embracing my hypocrisy – rejoicing in the consumption of meat yet condemning those who slaughter wildlife – I'm unfit to apprehend showboating the prey openly. People are strange, that's apparent. I slept with a kinky goth chick long ago. Her BDSM dungeon contained bushels of taxidermic ravens. Loyal Edgar Allen Poe fanatic perhaps. Ill-advisedly, I sought subsidiary information respecting the preserved birds fetish. She countered utilizing lewd comedy.

"What's the difference between taxidermy and a girl boinking?" Wednesday Addams submitted as I squirmed, fearful of the punchline. "One gets stuffed and mounted, the other gets mounted and stuffed." Then she necessitated I pinion her arms and yoke on a ball gag. Such a babe.

I gallivant toward a baroque cedar cabinet spotlighting black-and-white publicity photos of the *Giant* actors. I'm awestruck by an adolescent Dennis Hopper. A far cry from the "patron saint of deranged" he'd develop into. Thank God for drugs and alcohol. Across the hall, there's a memorabilia repository dedicated to the movie, replete with publications, apparel, images, and a life-size standee of the silver screen's legendary libertine.

The contiguous corridor introduces an all-encompassing gift shop, selling everything from postcards to jewelry and a hodgepodge of Marfa-themed trinkets. I select a candle, necklace, and tote for el jefe. Moderately generic yes, but she'll undoubtedly laud the effort. Settling the tab, I scour a rack of nostalgic hotel key chains engraved with the name of a cast member and the room number they lodged in. I add the **JAMES DEAN 223** pendant to my purchases. Oddly enough, Darby's fondness surpasses mine, so this'll serve as an invaluable prize and much more economical than the Esperanza jacket.

I rewind to the restaurant. It's called **JETT'S GRILL**, of course. I ask the brown-skinned barkeep for a spicy bloody, and he imparts that if the hunger pangs are in effect, I should nosh on their Texas Poutine – green chile gravy, caramelized onions, and bacon slopped over french-fried taters. Get in my belly!

While the kitchen staff rustles up my rations, I pass the time flirting with Zoe and Darby. It's not sexting per se because the correspondences aren't risqué. Conversely, Darby sends me a huge, uncircumcised schlong pic she received from an unlikely suitor. I marvel at the girth. I recap my trip, and they talk about this and that and how they're excited for me to come home. Tejano Moe Szyslak reemerges, transporting the Canadian delicacy. A single whiff later, I'm drowned in the starchy, sauce-soaked swine conflation, cutting off any external communication.

HITCHCOCK

It's half past drunk when I hobble out of Paisano after upgrading from the tomato-based elixir to bourbon after bourbon after bourbon before capping it off with, you guessed it – one concluding bourbon. Luckily, the poutine sopped up a pinch of the mash. That which perseveres implores me to keep on truckin'. Oppositely, my besotted anatomy campaigns for a catnap. Faltering through the Saint George, I traipse by reception and the happy hour brigade en route to Suite 313. I don't bother disrobing as I catapult atop the bed and...

The dream propagates like a silent film. My mother seated in the passenger side of a car, goggling the luxuriant shrubbery. Her husband sits behind, agitation raging. His hands are fumbling to harness the latch. Heeding the disturbance, mom's jowl moves – the announcement inaudible. Dad glances upward and rebuts – the dialogue muted. She unhooks and reaches into the rear. He tries to force her back. As the altercation persists, my father's observance deviates from his wife toward the windshield. His irises enlarge, and dread washes over him. With mouth agape, the solo aural resonance is a guttural scream.

DINNER FOR SCHMUCK

I rouse groggy and coerce my limbs upright. I'm peckish. I have a booking at Cochineal yet am reasonably assured I shouldn't venture before an audience. There's a strong chance I'm still blitzed. Hold on a sec, let me verify. Yessiree. I swipe the in-house dining menu from the workspace and call to order.

Awaiting delivery, I ingest a few Advil and try to crap the booze out. Maybe a shower would rejuvenate my exuberance. Nothing's hampering me. Room service isn't punctual. Inside the decontamination lavatory I proceed. Minutes afterward, I'm… mediocre at best but clean as a whistle.

Studying my entertainment options exposes it's slim pickings, underscoring the presumption I could easily piddle in my sweats. However, George Michael's anthemic "Freedom! '90" thumps through my internal Discman. Neglecting that the megastar recorded one of the greatest pop tracks hitherto, he was incorrect about a fundamental axiom – the clothes, do indeed, *always* make the man. Resultantly, I dress to impress – indigo Double RL western, black Todd Snyder jeans, and grey Varvatos Morrison Sharpeis. As I'm lacing up my boots, there's a knock at the door.

The waiter wheels in a cart, then bails. I yank off the lids and munch. Got real fancy and requested the crispy chicken sandwich, swapping the broccoli or soup for a wedge. The breaded fowl is moist and juicy. Teamed with dijonnaise, pickles, and slaw on brioche, transforms this Chick-fil-A forgery into a heavyweight contender. Whichever chef initially unified iceberg lettuce, bleu cheese and bacon crumbles deserved the James Beard Award. It never disappoints. I oughta replenish my electrolytes by means of Gatorade or Brawndo. In preference, I opt for a cocktail the hotel titles Ranch Water: blanco tequila, Topo Chico, lime, and a Tajín rim. Dios mío, that's dynamite! The devil's nectar spooks most gringos, but it's been asserted online tequila is the exclusive spirit that's an upper.

Although not scientifically proven, are you seriously going to rely on a physician's avowal instead of Reddit? Pshaw. Furthermore, I covet a stamina boost, and I've yet to unearth any coke. I demolish the meal, crush the refreshment, and the pep in my step reinstates.

LONELY PONY

It's too early to see the lights and too late to accomplish anything save carousing. I might be turning into a lush, but I'm on holiday, so sod off, ya wankers. Four blocks down, Marfa's solitary year-round, stand-alone pub subsists. 'Tis a nice evening for a walk. I rarely walk. Amazingly, I'll walk.

I embed the AirPods and troll the music library, pursuing the quintessential tune. "The Sound of Silence" by Simon & Garfunkel seems apropos. Paul begins plucking the acoustic, and I spark a Parliament. It drapes from my lips, nicotine filtering into my lungs, while the Gotham natives duet in perfect harmony. The first seven lines are eerily autobiographical and supply me with an inexplicable sense of equanimity. Nearing the watering hole, the strumming slows, and the decisive chord reverberates as I take my last drag.

An ocean of trampled bottle caps blankets the gravel. A resplendent, rectangular lightbox austerely reading **BEER** in red neon brackets a lofty, atrophying pole. Dingy roller shades shield the multi-paned windows, negating a passerby's ability to witness whatever debauchery occurs interiorly. Above the tattered entrance, a pallid sign appended to the gable presents the **LOST HORSE SALOON**.

Upon entering, I'm brought to an abrupt arrest. Déjà vu. There's a payphone secured to the drywall. Oh no, I'm not falling for that. How's the proverb go? Fool me once, shame on you. Fool me twice, shame on T-Swizzle for concocting melodies this goddamn infectious! Swiftly, pun intended, I cleave the handle, ready to shake my rump from scratch! The vibration of a conventional dial tone suctions my zeal, and I hang up disconsolate. I mope past several frayed pool tables and plump onto a stool. A gangly, unshaven, ponytailed buckaroo outfitted in a Stetson and Stevie Ray Vaughan tee, abandons his chat to mosey over. He's the living embodiment of a fusion between Sam Elliott and the Alpha and Omega.

"What'll it be, hoss?" he poses gruffly.

"Corona and a shot of Casamigas," I supplicate. As he acquires the libations, I case the joint to gain a better lay of the land. Lou Reed's "Walk on the Wild Side" pulsates from the juke ironically. The limited patrons hum along. Absence of revelry is understandable given it's hardly 9:00 p.m. on the Lord's Day.

The furnishings promote a cantina meets dive quality. Longhorn skulls affixed skyward. Framed posters and articles regarding the establishment displayed throughout. A rickety player piano props against the Venetian plastered stucco, bordering a skimpy, makeshift stage. A Lone Star backdrop ties the room together. Cowboy Jesus returns and plants the glassware.

"Join me?" I entreat.

"You buyin'?"

"Wouldn't have mentioned it otherwise."

"Then don't mind if I do," he relates merrily, pouring himself a shot. We chink and gulp. I swig the pilsner as my new chum kicks off the banter. "Which part of the lower forty-eight you visiting from?"

"Midwest."

"Where'd ya fly to?"

"Drove."

"You shittin' me?"

"I shit you not."

"Eighteen, nineteen hours?"

"Twenty-two with fuel and piss."

"Dang, pardner. Catch any Z's?"

"Au contraire, mon ami. Caffeine and barbecue," I remark facetiously.

"Ain't no rest for the wicked," he contributes, reloading the shooters. "This one's on me." I nod respectfully, and we run it back.

"Anybody ev…?" I was poised to explore the striking resemblance toward the narrator from *The Big Lebowski* and the dude who died for your sins when he interrupts.

"Yep, heard it all." He winks revealingly, then half-questions, half-alleges, "You've been in here before, haven't cha?"

"Negative. Marfa virgin."

"Really? That's interesting because I would've testified on the King James I recognized you, and I almost always forget a face," he professes, grinning.

"HA! Tremendously overdue."

"Well, nothing changes around these parts, minus the clientele. Used ta be a quiet town 'til it became the numéro uno hashtag west of the Mississippi."

"Yeah, what provoked that?"

"Tale as old as mankind. An individual embarks on a quest for solitude and finds it, then makes the blunder of broadcasting their discovery. Word spreads like wildfire, and presto, you've got yourself a tourist destination. Similar to the fate that befell Austin. The only thing weird about ATX anymore is its shortage of weirdness."

"Lived here long?"

"Shucks, twenty plus years, I reckon. Let's just say yours truly arrived ahead of that swanky, counterfeit boutique. But Texas is all I've ever known."

"How so?"

"Born in Lubbock. Family moved to Amarillo when I was a tyke. Spent my teens outside Galveston. Did a stint in Huntsville. Wound up here post-parole, and here I have remained from that juncture forward. Come to think of it, haven't crossed the state line since I buried my momma in '09."

Unreal. I've circumnavigated the globe and don't feel I've found my place. This ex-con hasn't done dick yet comprehends precisely where he belongs.

"That's enough about me. How's about another round on you?"

"Deal," I concur, laughing. He refills the shots, and we deftly administrate the tequila triple play.

"What's on the docket tonight?" he probes.

I jingle the brewski and simper. "Scope out the lights at some point, also."

"In a hurry?"

"To get…?"

"Exactamundo. Time doesn't exist in this neck of the woods. My advice, sit tight. At 3 a.m., it'll be just you and the cosmos. No finer hour to search for the unknown."

"You believe in that drivel? Supernatural and aliens, and whatnot."

"Nah, the paranormal ain't my bag, brother. I've seen the mystery lights of Marfa and my fair share of other crazy-ass shit though. My pals and I would swing by the platform and drop acid. Those were the days. Heck, I'm unsure I've gone in damn near a decade, and them pals of mine are either residing in different zip codes or on permanent vacation." A conclave of yuppies invades, and my drinking buddy strays their way.

"Is it worth it?" I challenge.

He spirals and asks, "What's that?"

"The lights. Worth seeing?"

"Worth has many variables, my friend, but I can tell you this – the truth is out there, and if you seek it, it shall set you free," he portends ominously. And with a tipping of the brim, he rambles on.

Alrighty then. Now that I've gathered the lowdown from Creepy McCreeperson, I'll polish off my cerveza, zoom back to the hotel, and waste away in Margaritaville pre-siesta. **Mental note:** stop talking to strangers.

DARK SIDE OF THE MOON

My alarm buzzes at 2:45 a.m., and I strive to determine if this fable merits chasing or if staying under the sheets isn't the shrewder plan of attack. I lie inert, reminding myself I haven't driven 1400 miles to simply get liquored up and pass out in a hotel. Moreover, the famed Marfa Lights aren't a phenomena that can be experienced back home. So, by 2:50 a.m., I'm showering, <u>again</u>, flushing the booze, <u>again</u>. At 3:00 a.m., I'm toweled off, recalling it was in the high fifties earlier, but the forecast inferred it would dip below thirty at this interval. Due to that, I integrate long sleeves and a Levi's Sherpa into my sightseeing attire, then boogie.

I dismount the elevator, and the unduly, eager desk clerk — wax-tipped mustache and Oliver Peoples complementing his suspenders and neckerchief hipster accoutrements — aspires to chew the fat with the marginally soused, partially asleep, thoroughly irritable guest.

"Where you headed at this hour?" he pries.

"Off to see the wizard," I grumble irreverently.

"Eh?"

"The lights."

"Oh, wonderful. They're absolutely magical."

I scoff, soldier through the egress, and plop into the Benz. Clearing the cobwebs is incumbent, and I have supreme confidence Trent Reznor's the most qualified candidate for the job. Subsequently, I nominate Nine Inch Nails' "Mr. Self Destruct." Streaming it uproariously over the Burmester audio system frightens the dozing German. I grant her a moment to reanimate, then switch gears.

Eight miles down, I encounter the **MARFA LIGHTS VIEWING AREA 1 MILE** placard, and like clockwork, sixty seconds later, abracadabra. There's a plenitude of blacktop, but merely four legitimate parking spaces, each marked handicapped. As the friendly neighborhood bartender implied, nobody else is here, and odds of additional conspiracy theorists rolling up seem bleak. Therefore, I take the liberty of puncturing the forbidden zone, saying my prayers that a busload of senior citizens doesn't pop round and club the youth outta me.

A voluminous brick wall girdles the facility with staircases at both ends, a walkway in the middle, and an ADA compliant ramp, for good measure. Advancing on the cylindrical structure, I'm apprised bathrooms occupy the bulk of the square footage, leading me to surmise untold visitors bring intoxicants, and I damn well should've.

The elevated platform consists of alloyed benches aligned east to west, excess seating sections situated north and south, fringing a trifecta of anchored tower viewers that overlook the Chinati Mountains. A welded wire fencing delineates the premises from private property, extrapolated by the **NO TRESPASSING** sign.

Now what? I don't detect a glint, much less any mythical hocus-pocus. What's palpable – the grotesquely inclement twenty-six degrees Fahrenheit. Glad I imprudently forgot my beanie coupled with the bourbon at the Saint George. As a replacement, I flick the Bic on a cigarette, and expel into obscurity.

I'm captivated by the star coverage. A trillion itsy-bitsy clusters twinkling upon me. In retrospect, I haven't gazed toward the firmament this often during my lifetime. It's so contradictory to all that I am, yet so utterly majestic. The ember smolders to the filter, and I'm stoked to give it a whirl.

I lean into the binoculars. Something's wrong, I can't see anything. Sussing out whether quarters are compulsory to operate this gizmo, I ascertain there isn't a change slot. Putz. I glom the leaden hull, then rabidly wave my idle hand in front of the lens. Boom baby! I jockey laterally to garner a basic knowledge and master the craft forthwith. The geography magnifies infinitely and a sector ninety klicks off appears centimeters away. Conundrum being, I have no effing idea where I'm supposed to target. Consequently, I aim toward Mexico and hope for the best.

Time tiptoes laggardly as I've glowered at emptiness for ages. I'm growing weary, and my level of self-reproach has multiplied. Why'd I ditch the comfort of the bed? The lack of exhilaration renders me acutely conscious of the climate, and I blow hot air inside my cupped fists to thaw. The condensed vapor siphons through my palms like tobacco smoke, wafting into the glacial breeze.

Even though it's 4:30 a.m. wherever Darby's inevitably fornicating, I ping her. *Hola. Super annoyed. At the Marfa Lights. Complete sham and it's ducking freezing. About to cry myself to sleep.* Beautifully written if I may be so bold. Especially imputing my frozen opposable digits. But how come autocorrect converts 'fuck' to 'duck' without exception? C'mon, Apple, step up your game. With zero reply imminent, I bite the bullet.

I angle into the eyepiece and scan the region. Guiding the apparatus tardily, I discern a beam from my peripheral. I jerk the glasses and spot a yellowish-whitish orb dancing. Then another unveils itself, and another. An accumulation levitates. Others are swaying and… Shit! They've evanesced. Tease. I need more. Keep alert. Eyes peeled. You nev…

An orphan ray flourishes, then a second and a third. There's a fourth and a fifth traveling in opposing directions. Holy Moses! Two of them bond, then break apart. A few slither snakelike. Synchronically, a constellation floats cloudward. I surveil an isolated sphere and swivel. But they dematerialize instanter. Smiling radiantly, I flame a P Funk and wallow in my success. I've seen the Marfa Lights, and nothing could've prepared me for the joy I'm inheriting. It's euphoric. I've waited an eternity to sample this, and that resoluteness is paying dividends substantially.

I compose a follow-up message to Darby. *Delete the previous text. They're incredible! Wish you were here. Kisses.* I tuck my cell and extinguish the cig, chomping at the bit. I'm hooked. I resume inspection. The lights immediately recrudesce.

All of a sudden, my hand slips, and the binoculars stagger downward. My vision cuts across the desolate tract, and I recoil straightaway. Dafuq was that?! Some type of dormant animal? My breathing hastens, heart palpitating savagely. I prowl forward to examine afresh, methodically shifting along the plateau. As I hone in on the creature, I croak harrowingly. Am I hallucinating? I peer into the gloom to corroborate if what I'm perceiving is real. It's too dim to validate with any grade of certainty. I restore my position, cautiously dissecting the habitat until…

That wasn't an animal – it's a human being. I leap off the platform, iPhone flashlight deployed to peregrinate through the void. Verging upon the fence, I hurdle the top rail and rocket onward, twigs snapping, foliage crackling under my shoes. A stifled moan ventilates, and the wailing intensifies with every clomp. I'm approximately forty yards out when I draw to a screeching halt. My bones tremor as I kneel on the grass. The body lies prostrate, arms splayed, shirt drenched in gore.

"Sir, can you hear me?" No answer. "I'm gonna dial 911." No response. I prospect the acreage to evaluate where he originated from. There's barrenness for miles, and noting his condition, I'm skeptical of the extent he could have trekked. It's tenable there's a ranch in the vicinity, but none I'm able to pinpoint. Without warning, he coughs twice, and I jolt backward, horrified.

"Help. Help me," the man petitions feebly.

I'm quavering as I inch closer. "Okay, I'll call the cops and…"

"No. No cops."

"We've gotta rush you to a hospital. You require medical attention."

"They're coming."

"Who? Who's coming?" I ask, teeth chattering.

"The men that did this. They want the key."

"What? What men? What key? If we don't get you assistance soon, you'll… You're hemorrhaging a…"

He hoists his head, and I stare, aghast. His tissue so mutilated even his own mother couldn't identify him. Pure terror spans the remnants. "Listen carefully," he prescribes. "There's a bus station in Dallas. Locate the room of lockers. Hidden behind number thirteen is an envelope containing a key. It unlocks the door. Do not…" He hacks thunderously, and sanguine goo spills onto the soil. I retch and nearly vomit. The man staves off the misery to endure. "Do not let them confiscate the parcel."

"What's inside the locker?" I beseech tentatively. He doesn't react. "What's inside the locker, sir?!" I holler.

"The missing link," he whispers, respiratory organs battling for oxygen.

"Huh? I don't… There's still time to…"

"There is no time. You must go."

I digest the words yet am incapable of processing the ultimatum. I'm stuck in intellectual quicksand – legs debilitated while I sink into purgatory.

He conjures the last of his fortitude and shrieks, "GO! GO NOW!!!"

The commandment resuscitates my faculties, and I spring to action. I'm in an all-out sprint toward the barrier. Perspiration secreting from my pores. I launch into orbit, clasp the wiring, and vault over. I stick the landing, hustle around the building, and barge inside the coupe. I smash the starter, then burn rubber.

As I blast onto the road, my sneaker intuitively crashes to the floorboard, and I'm racing mortality through the cooling twilight. Adrenaline has fully taken hold. Slow the fuck down. Can't get stopped. I ease off the throttle, reducing to 75… 65… 55… 40… 30.

Edging toward the blinking signal, I pause, turn onto Highland, and stiffen. Across the alley of my hotel, an insignia extruding from a tinted storefront at the City Hall complex publicizes the **MARFA POLICE DEPARTMENT**. How'd I miss that? I kill the ignition at the adjacent post office and scud for the Saint George.

"Welcome bah…," the receptionist hails. I zap past him mid-salutation.

At the elevator, I wallop the up arrow ceaselessly, speculating my hysteria might prompt the cab faster than normal. The gate separates, and I burst in, knuckle soldered to the close button. The meddlesome twat progresses, then studies me, raddled. Discourse is unnecessary; my countenance speaks volumes. The jaws unite, and I ascend.

Desisting on three, the portal unshackles ploddingly, but I'm already lunging out. I rake my pockets, grip the plastic card, and stretch for the RFID electronic mortise. Access authorized. Instantaneously, I rotate the dead bolt, slide the chain, then ram my pupil into the peephole, oscillating helter-skelter. Vacant. I recede to the dresser, unload my possessions, and roam cyclonically.

What should I do? Notify the authorities? Fuck! The man specified no cops. Maybe they're accomplices. Think. Think dammit! Did I touch him? There'd be fingerprints. I don't remember. Were there security cameras? I didn't notice any. Then again, I wasn't on the lookout. Can anyone place me at the scene of the crime? Crap! The nimrod downstairs could instruct the detectives we spoke upon decampment, and I returned wholly discombobulated. That lends credibility to my potential involvement, right? At the very minimum, it's grounds for interrogation and detainment in this Godforsaken town. What about the Lost Horse bartender? It isn't far-fetched to conceive a felonious assault began with beverages at the lone tavern. And presuming he antes up our powwow accompanied by his suggested arrival, guilt will decidedly point to me!

I'm reviewing the fiasco on loop. It unfailingly reverts to the same thing – that man in the field. The drubbing he sustained and those eyes, those unnerving, demoralized eyes. I'll be haunted by them forever. And who are these barbarians that levied the mercilessness? He swore they were coming. Does his elimination denote I've become their fill-in scapegoat? How would they know? Would he snitch? If you torture somebody enough, they'd eventually confess to assassinating JFK.

Rife with angst, rapidly losing control of my mind, I cannonball into the mini bar, excavating the airplane bottles of whiskey and guzzling them headlong. When they're depleted, I grab whatever I can – tequila, gin, scotch, vodka. I'm on my haunches, chugging the spirits, one after the next, until the fridge has emptied.

I wager to stand and wobble awkwardly, reaching for the chair. It teeters sideways, and we hit the dirt. I claw at the console and lug myself vertically. My brain's fractured, and delirium sets in. I glimpse a cherry liquid trickling from the ceiling. The flow increases and streaks down the walls. I deflect my diligence expecting it'll evaporate, yet I'm convinced droplets are splattering onto the desk. I plug my ears to no avail as the pitter-patter amplifies. I reappraise, and the liquid is spurting riotously, then ricochets off the varnish and coats me. What's happening?!

Without hesitation, I undress and scuttle into the bathroom, into the shower, into the arctic waters, letting them cascade over me. Slumped atop that absurd wooden stool, I knead my temples to assuage the distress. It's an act of futility. The temperature warms and I rise bewildered. There's no blood: not on my skin, not in the drain, not a trace anywhere. I slope against the enamel, replaying the grisly confrontation.

I hop out and wrap a robe around me. Scrambling back to the bedroom, I tumble onto the comforter. That impaired voice perfuses my psyche – 'Dallas. Bus station. Lockers. Thirteen. Envelope. Key.' It doesn't add up. My eyelids grow heavy, extremities anesthetized as exhaustion and liquor ooze through my capillaries. I essay to repel it. There are so many obstacles demanding abolition, but they're exiled into temporary adjournment because the tribulation subsides, and I fade to black.

THIS IS NOT AN EXIT

The landline rings and doesn't ebb. "H-H-Hello?" I stutter groggily.

"Hello, sir, this is Nicholas at the front desk. I'm confirming today's departure."

"Yeah, just a little longer."

"Well, sir, it's 1:00 in the afternoon, and…"

"What?! Shit!" I discard the receiver, then flounder across my early morning bedlam, totally disoriented. Expeditiously, I throw on fresh garb and cram my belongings into the backpack. I sling the straps around my shoulders, poach the hanging items and toiletries, and scat.

Illumination from the hallway greets me harshly as I rampage toward the elevator. The room door thuds shut, and a twosome twirls to monitor. I forge aloofly and the three of us ingress. Once our descent initiates, I visualize addled looks being exchanged, enhancing my trepidation. I've yet to construct anything resembling a strategy, and surely one won't crystallize anterior to this ride culminating. My windpipe constricts, and I start panting like an overheated dog. I'm a prisoner inside this steel death trap, plummeting into my personal Hell. The woman pats me palliatively and asks if I'm sick. I don't comment. I'm not trying to be rude; I quite literally cannot verbalize speech. I squeeze my thighs, wheezing dementedly. Both passengers are addressing me, but it's incoherent. The brakes tauten, and the elevator grinds to suspension. I transplant my aspect, expression of a true American psycho etched across my face. The pair evacuates on the double. I dawdle, hands strangling the banister. When the coast is clear, I slink over the sill and dwell in the vestibule, pixilated.

Roving hazily, I'm hamstrung by the appearance of two uniformed officers looming at registration. I backpedal full tilt and hide behind the paneling. FUUUUUUUUUUCK!!! As I pirouette, ferreting for a plan B, I recollect custodians smoking on the stoop of a service entry between the lounge and restaurant yesterday. With no other alternatives, I make my escape.

I scurry down the corridor and almost bulldoze a waitress hauling a tray of dishes. She stops short to skirt the collision. I lengthen my arms and push strenuously. Locked! I bow in capitulation, clenching the crossbar.

"Excuse you!" the lady hisses angrily.

I skulk past her and glance at the patrolmen debriefing a shrouded employee. Screw it. The only way is through. I unzip the Tortuga and don my Tom Ford combo to effectuate a cloak of invisibility. Checkout time.

My ligaments are Jell-O, but I propel them into motion. Seventy-five feet... Fifty feet... Twenty-five feet... And then... Instinct assumes jurisdiction, and I nervously pivot. The clerk's engrossment digresses. Our optics bind. He gawks in a state of shock, lips pursed, primed to rat me to the pigs. Before he has the opportunity, I surge onto the sidewalk.

Stampeding up the avenue, I nab the fob and click. I bombard the rental, chucking the paraphernalia into the back seat. I peel out, bust a right at East Lincoln, then defy the octagonal traffic edict, powersliding onto Russell. Three blocks south, I bang a left, breach the main thoroughfare, and prognosticate amnesty. Then and there it dawns I'm inhabiting the most conspicuous getaway car in the annals of getaways. I'm a sitting duck.

The speed limit is 30 mph, and I struggle to maintain. Gaining on the 40-mph marker, I heed the rearview – nada. As 55 mph surfaces, my perusal's fused to the district ahead – diddly. 65 mph placard sprouts, and I'm gyrating maniacally – zilch. 75 mph incoming, and I punch it, sailing along U.S. 90 East at a breakneck pace with Marfa practically erased.

Moments from the viewing area advisory I mull my choices. It all boils down to this – park and sleuth or keep motoring? Hmph. The hypothetical ramifications outweigh the upsides. Choking the steering wheel at ten and two, I rev up to 8000 rpm. As the platform approaches, I reconnoiter surreptitiously. No signs of life. There is, however, a black Cadillac.

It could be nothing. It could be everything. It's irrelevant nonetheless because I clobber the gas, leaving the town in the dust. I'm fifteen miles outside Alpine, and I have a feeling if I can pass through without incident, I'll succeed in putting this whole mess behind me. But there's still the issue of Dallas and John Doe's final request.

PROTECTION

The velocity of my thoughts is dizzying. It's implausible to concentrate on something other than the current predicament. There's no radio, no iTunes, no audiobook. The scant noises are the rumble of the road, the whipping of the wind, and the ingrained pronouncements of an anonymous cripple.

Although going home as quickly as possible represents the smartest move, swirling reminiscences of my father have me voyaging toward Dallas. I grasp exactly which measures he'd adopt under these circumstances, and that's the motivating factor behind this hugely, unintelligent detour. The guy boasted an unparalleled benevolence, whereas my philanthropy has been confined to tax write-offs. And while it'd be a piece of cake extending that selfishness, once again, his memory prohibits it. How long would I wrestle with regret if I played it safe? I haven't the slightest what I'm walking into but should brace for whatever awaits.

I can't use a gun. Dad wouldn't approve of them and had me promise I'd abide by that same tenet. When I balked, he made things abundantly evident this wasn't a plea, it was an ordinance. Constant appeals to divulge his rationale were contested with a prosaic four-syllable elucidation – "They are lethal." I divined it rather hypocritical considering he served his country, and last I heard, the armed forces mandated firearms expertise for their troops. Hence, I felt ulterior agendas prevailed. The world's full of deadly devices. Why did this warrant such a behest? He eschewed telling me, and those rebuttals aren't forthcoming. Regardless, it's a moot point. I took an oath, and I won't renege on that.

No heater equals no weapon. Acknowledging a knife, taser, or golf club each depict viable substitutes, I've omitted one small detail. Despite commanding an inscrutable knack for ruffling feathers, I've never actually engaged in hand-to-hand combat. I suppose that's attributable to the fact I'm adept at talking my ass out of every jam.

So, where does that leave us? What're my strengths aside from bullshitting? Admitting a scenario that rivals this is entirely foreign to me, I'd say my advantages over prospective foes include superior aptitude, fleetness of foot, and driving prowess.

Typically, I'm cunning enough to outwit most opponents, but after the recent occurrences, my gray matter has mushed. Decades removed from the high school track days, notwithstanding, I'm fit as a fiddle and do cardio regularly. That said, I've puffed more tar than the Marlboro Man lately, thus outdistancing anybody sounds improbable; ergo, survival may depend upon my handling of this imported machine, provided the situation degenerates. When it comes to fight-or-flight, I'm on the run like O.J. Difference being the Bronco didn't wield the horsepower of the Mercedes and getting caught isn't an option.

DEEP ELLUM BLUES

Beyond the horizon, the shapes of awe-inspiring, architectural wonders burgeon across the skyline. The Reunion Tower's mesmerizing LED ball, alongside the sheer enormity and grandeur of the effulgent Bank of America Plaza, pave the way, infusing a vibrancy to downtown Dallas. As I hover above the Trinity River, I'm enthralled with the symmetry of the Margaret McDermott Bridge and its inimitable pomp. Twin arches supported by gargantuan cables rank this overpass among the classiest I've ever traversed. The Waze app informs me that the off-ramp is nigh, and my clarity rebounds. Though I wish there was time to tour this glamorous metroplex, I'm not here to see the sights. I'm here for one reason, and one reason alone.

I exit the freeway and circle the station. A meter frees up, and I glide in. My butt is cemented to the saddle – I'm petrified. What are you doing, jackass? Tepidly, I trudge into the waiting area. It reeks of urine, and the larger portion of the occupants make my skin crawl. It's a hobo convention. I'm definitely out of my element, Donny. A ticketing agent routes me to self-storage, and I bob and weave, spurning contact with the vermin.

Two junkies loiter in the space, sharing a baggy of crystalline powder. I dither and sweep the perimeter, scrounging for anything unusual. Any indication I've been followed. Any guards clocking me. Any seedy characters exempting those I've already observed, that is. There are zero immediate threats, and nobody gives a shit. The vagrants skedaddle, and I penetrate, scouting for unlucky thirteen.

Tension percolates as I squat and press my ear to the armor – silence. I pad to the edge of the tier. The unit rests flush against the wall. I glue my fingernails onto the frame and tug with every fiber of my being. They slip off, and I jet in reverse, docking hard on the linoleum, writhing. Rallying the minimal vigor that perdures, I pick myself up and judge whether my valiant effort did the trick.

Roughly six inches of clearance is all I could induce, but that's adequate to note the envelope taped to the rear. I lodge my arm into the gap, hooking my pinkie around the strip, and excise it from constraint.

I thread the envelope toward me, tear the side fold, and, with palm outspread, collar the key. We've reached the point of no return. What's in store… that's anyone's guess. I suspire. My hand twitches, inserting the brass into the cylinder. Gingerly, I turn it, lift the lever, and take a peek – it's another plain white mailer. I forage the interior to affirm I haven't glossed over something. A pedestrian intrudes, and I stuff the envelope down my pants, then abscond.

I whisk to the coupe and inspect the wrapper intently. There's nothing peculiar whatsoever. I shovel underneath the seal, severing the adhesive, and pry the innards. Confusion reigns as I procure three Polaroids and a voucher of sorts. The first photo displays Prada Marfa featuring a significantly dulled date. I can barely translate the sequence. To the best of my capabilities, I've deduced twelves on the fringes and a twenty halfway. WTF? The second portrays the Presidio County Courthouse. The month, day, and year are more legible, albeit smudged. I decipher a twelve, a twenty-three, and a fourteen. My pulse throbs, sanity on the threshold of devastation. I'm lightheaded. I sip the water before assessing the third snapshot. It's the *Giant* mural, dated 12/24/18. The numerals less consequential than the handwriting itself.

I fan out the pictures like a Japanese sensu, scrutinizing each meticulously. An epiphany seeps into my neurons, and I rip open the glove box, then exhume the envelope filled during my trip. I extract miscellaneous Polaroids cohering them in the opposite hand, inquiry fixated on the borders, locomoting between both groups. My pupils dilate, trachea compresses. The film falls from my clutches as my arms quiver tumultuously. I hoick the door handle and puke onto the concrete. With crown drooping, torso leaning toward the curb, I miraculously manage to drag myself back.

It's a match. The penmanship spattering the bus depot imagery perfectly imitates the conglomeration I recently acquired in Marfa. A fierce ripple of panic courses internally. I can't catch my breath. I imbibe the remainder of the water, hoping to regain composure. It's a forlorn attempt. I'm calm like a bomb. Darby taught me a relaxation exercise. Inhale through my nostrils, counting to four. Exhale through my mouth, counting to four. One one-thousand, two one-thousand, three one-thousand, four one-thousand, sniff. One one-thousand, two one-thousand, three one-thousand, four one-thousand, expire. Repeat.

I begin to stabilize, yet the questions linger. Whose photos are these? Why were they inside that locker? How the hell does the scrawl duplicate mine? My glare lops to the floor mat.

LUGGAGE CLAIM CHECK
5712-19

NAME

1

NUMBER OF BAGS

THE PEABODY MEMPHIS

I invert the stub, uncovering a liability disclaimer and an address. Lightning bolts shoot across my pallium. Bemused, I tap a Parliament from the pack, ruminating over a multitude of ostensible backstories. I've traveled to Memphis, Tennessee, on numerous occasions. Elvis Presley lived there. Jeff Buckley died there. Johnny Cash recorded there. Bluff City is steeped in rich music history. But I have never stayed at this hotel. Never even visited. Never had an incentive to do so… until now.

THE INSOMNIAC BEAVER

I've audited the Polaroids endlessly since deserting the terminal. I need answers, yet there's greater than four hundred miles preceding the next batch of clues on this nonsensical scavenger hunt. Having been so distracted by all that's arisen, I ignored how low the tank has gotten – out of the frying pan, into the fire.

Signage for Royse City emerges. A whopping cartoon rodent glitters overhead. Riveted, I pilot toward it, exposing the most enormous gas station I've ever witnessed. I'm estimating there's sixty pumping islands lining the pavement. Ninety-nine percent are populated. A Ducati finishes up, and I feed my voracious chariot. I too am famished but grouchy and haggard, as well. Not an ideal threesome, and one that must be rectified pronto.

While the car glugs fuel, I tramp to the showroom. Mountainous crimson letters herald the title **BUC-EE'S**. Wandering indoors, I'm entranced by the colossal nature of my environment. Undisputedly, *everything* is bigger in Texas. Virtually a soccer pitch diametrically, it's packed to the gills and divided into two domains. The west wing accentuates provisions – an unabridged jerky section, aisles bristling with candies and snacks, and an unlawful quota of sodas. To the east, an outlet akin to a Walmart, tendering souvenirs, household goods, and playthings. I infiltrate arguably the nation's largest and cleanest public restroom – in the ballpark of forty urinals and stalls, every square inch sparkling. Where the devil am I?

After taking care of business, I choose to dine pre-syncope. Browsing the unlimited possibilities, I'm dumbfounded they roast pecans and almonds and smoke meats onsite. I order a chopped beef sandwich and brisket taco, and they're assembled in a flash. Retreating to the pump, I wolf them down, disconnect the hose, and slap the hatch.

I'm ready to scarper when I clap onto a darkened automobile due north. It's awfully emblematic of the sedan from the viewing platform mere hours ago. A male quartet suited in black, ivory shirts, and skinny ties sits within. Each wearing sunglasses at night, like Corey Hart, gazing in my general proximity. What're they looking at? I squinny over my shoulder. A bunch of critters are defecating on the lawn, and a faction of teenagers congregate around a cooler. My heedfulness defaults to the cast of *Reservoir Dogs*. The driver's limb is projected outward. He aims his index and middle fingers at my skull, concurrently raising his thumb and tweaking it precipitately in the same vein as firing a pistol. The commissures of his lips curl, producing a spine-chilling grin.

Instantly, I storm the CLA and put the pedal to the metal. The Caddy's headlights electrify, and the fearsome foursome tails me along the frontage road. I torpedo onto the interstate, then skew into the fast lane, accelerating to 80 mph. My eyes alternate between the asphalt and rearview, laboring to keep them in the crosshairs. How the fuck did they triangulate me? The wheelman slaloms through the congestion with the precision of a downhill skier. My shoe plunges, and I surpass 100 mph, swerving into the center lane then back, blazing past an orange Corvette. I'm a solid twenty-five miles above the legal restriction but worrying about the fuzz is negligible. I redline the engine, maneuvering nimbler than Mario Andretti. Exploring the side mirrors continually, my pursuers lag farther and farther behind until they've dropped off the radar. That's of minor reassurance because pulling over isn't in the cards. My suspected homicide will facilitate perseverance for the foreseeable future.

GIMME SHELTER

I'm two hours from Memphis, and drowsiness is saturating briskly. My arm lolls out the window, vying to remain vigil as the staleness of the air gusts everywhere. It's feasible I could nurse a cup of coffee, torch another cigarette, and journey onward. Instead, I conclude repose sagest. I navigate toward a Podunk town called Lonoke, nestled thirty miles east of Little Rock in the Razorback State. There are copious prospects, but a poorly maintained motel distinguishes itself. The decaying marquee supplies comedic relief on this highly unamusing evening. A tercet of witty prose heaped one below the other yucks:

COLOR TV – COURTESY INTERWEBS
PETS WELCOME – WE ARE HUNGRY
HAVE YOUR NEXT AFFAIR WITH US

The word **VACANCY** scintillates beneath in neon. I chuckle at the corniness and commit to a thorough analysis. The exterior clamors for a paint job, and the yard would benefit from some landscaping, amidst a plenitude of supplemental renovations. All in all, it leaves a lot to be desired, yet I turn a deaf ear to my mother's voice complaining about such a rathole. Nobody anticipates a European luxury vehicle at an abode of this obscene caliber, and there's not a ghost of a chance my mysterious assailants search here.

"Forty-two flat, tax included. Cash or credit?" the old codger, brandishing a raggedy flannel and jeans, asks.

"Um, which do you prefer?" I consult, nonplussed. Then it registers that when there aren't amenities and zippo worth stealing, monetary collateral becomes trivial.

"Cash is king," he touts with a near-toothless smile.

"Then cash it is, my friend. Can I get a room where I won't be bothered?" I cajole, handing him a Ulysses.

"Easy peasy. We're a bit light tonight. I'll put ya in the honeymoon suite," he cackles. "Just a tinge of motel shenanigans."

"Like your marquee, huh?"

"Yes indeedy. Dreamt them up myself. The missus and I been squabbling over it. What's yer opinion?"

"Brilliant marketing ploy."

"Much obliged, Yankee. Told that Jezebel we gotsta outfox the competitors to attract customers. She lacks gumption. That's why I chain her in the attic," he wisecracks, then wrenches a key off the knob and lofts it across the counter.

"You're a funny guy."

"I ain't Jack Benny, but jokes are my forte."

"Au revoir," I impart hospitably.

"Sleep tight… Don't let the bed bugs bite!" he shouts wryly, and I blanch.

Accessing the fleabag, I fling the chenille quilt onto the shag. Even though the local yokel was messing with me, I'm erring on the side of caution. I configure multiple alarms, then crater atop the moth-ravaged polyester, fully clothed.

BURDEN IN MY HAND

I skate into the valet at 10:57 a.m. and disembark – an attendant is already inbound. "Keep it close. I'll be out in a quick," I purport, palming him a sawbuck before bustling through the ornate doorway.

The lobby's a mob scene. Droves of people, varied sizes, pigments, and generations dillydallying. It's pandemonium. Everybody hyped for… I haven't the foggiest. Prior to investigating, a John Philip Sousa concerto thunders over the speakers, and the swarm simmers. Their absorption transposes toward the atrium. I jostle for positioning to attain a clearer view. They've rolled a red carpet along the tile, stretching to an illustrious, marble fountain. A miniature set of stairs unifies them.

A gentleman parading a three-quarter length, maroon sport coat with gold tassels culled from the Napoleon Bonaparte war anthology exits the elevator. A grey pinstriped vest disguises the alabaster dress shirt and burgundy polka-dotted tie. Ebony trousers imbricating congruous derbies round out the ensemble. He strides down the runway, swinging a mahogany cane, and the crowd goes wild. Confounded by this solo fashion show, I nudge closer. Five mallard ducks waddle in front. Spectators capture photographs and videos, ogling wondrously. The Naomi, Cindy, Linda, Christy, and Claudia of the aquatic bird modeling world strut their stuff, unfazed. Individually, they advance, prance up the steps, then pogo into the basin. A prepubescent girl crouches at my feet, howling.

"Explain this to me," I necessitate.

She frowns patronizingly. "It's the duck march. Doy! They live on the roof, and every morning the Duckmaster gets them out of their palace to swim. Then, at 5:00 p.m., he leads them upstairs for the night. It's so neat."

I giggle at the cuteness and momentarily forget why I'm here. The horde disperses, and she scrams. I interface with the concierge, clarifying where packages are retrieved. He chaperones me to the bellhop podium.

An affable nitwit named Isaiah receives me. "Greetings, sir. May I help you?"

I furnish the perforated cardboard, mum. He appraises it, and a flustered look germinates. "There a problem?" I grill.

"It's, erm… This is twelve months old, theoretically older."

"How can you tell?"

"You see that series of numbers?" He points at the 5712-19. "The nineteen's the year. It'd be a miracle for us to still have this in our possession."

"Why?" I drill frustratingly.

"I'm just a trainee, but quite sure we dispose of articles when they aren't collected after a designated period. Let me locate my supervisor," he announces, then skitters away.

Venom frothing, migraine forming. I've read the fine print. They're contractually required to release the product to anyone presenting the ticket. But what if he's correct? What if they "lost" it or trashed it or insist I pay for the inconvenience of holding onto it? As I'm contemplating the what ifs, Isaiah returns.

"Mr. Graham will join us soon."

A grizzled black man sidles up, cradling a vintage leather briefcase, replicating the style that transported Marsellus Wallace's soul in *Pulp Fiction*. His free hand tinkers with an identification tag embossed **KENON**. Sauntering behind the podium, he murmurs to his subordinate, and the protégé bids us adieu.

Kenon hefts the container atop the ledge and transfers his concern to me, devoid of any sentiment. His temperament casually evolves into jolliness. "I sincerely didn't expect you'd come back. 363 days later, alakazam. The fellas and I had a bet. You cost me fifty bucks. Well, fifty-two technically, seeing that you're a couple days early," Kenon enlightens, withdrawing a bundle of bills. He peels off the singles, then lays them on the husk.

I gape, categorically flummoxed. "Sorry, I'm not following. Whaddaya mean, 'come back?' "

His gaiety shrivels, stumped by my inquisition. "Is this a game, sir? I ain't very good at games."

"You said you didn't 'expect' me to 'come back.' Have we met?"

"Uh, yes, sir. You left this briefcase with me last December. Vowed you'd claim it in a year. Offered me a dollar per day. The money's the only reason I consented. Being the holidays and all, figured I'd buy my sugar an extra special gift. I stored this beaut inside my cubby the whole time. Couldn't trust sticking it in the baggage closet unattended. Property held more than a few weeks, a month tops, gets donated or destroyed, but priceless relics such as yours get 'misplaced.' They don't weather the gluttony of crooked men. Anfernee's Pawnshop got these fools on retainer. Greedy bastards."

My fever's rising, sweat beads drizzling from my glands. What's this dinosaur talking about? Beyond a shadow of a doubt, I've never seen him. And I've unequivocally never entered this hotel. "Are you positive it was me? Maybe you've mistaken me with someone else."

His joviality morphs into contempt. He scooches forward and lowers his tone a shade. "Listen here, youngblood. I've worked at The Peabody almost thirty-five years and haven't skipped a shift. You honestly think it's difficult ID'ing the punk who paid my black ass to stash a briefcase for an entire year? As though that's common practice. Sheeit, you one crazy mofo. I'd recommend you quash whicheva kinda stunt you're fixin' to pull and get the lead out. Ya dig?"

Like Christopher Walken in *True Romance*, I'm resolving if Mr. Kenon Graham is lying by examining him head to toe. He's speaking the truth – or at least believes so – yet it's impossible. Wooziness pervades, and my knees crumple.

"Hey chief, you okay?" he prods, vacating his post to straighten me.

I sneer at him and retort, "I'm pretty fucking far from okay." I clinch the handgrip and stomp away as the George Washingtons float languishingly.

The valet spots me, tunnels through the drawer, and tosses the fob. I dump the attaché on the passenger seat, then jog around the hood. My progression terminated at the sight of the sedan butted against my bumper. The motorist thrusts a fist under his chin, protracts the thumb, and simulates slashing his Adam's apple.

I nosedive into the Mercedes and hightail it onto the street. With reckless abandon, I make a U-turn, nearly sideswiping a trolley. Belligerent honks thrum at me as I whizz down Union Avenue toward Riverside and discover placards for I-40 West. Approaching the on-ramp, I blow a red light, narrowly evading a southbound minivan. The speedometer eclipses 90 mph over the Hernando de Soto Bridge. Whooshing past the mastodonic **Bass Pro Shops Pyramid**, I screen the **WELCOME TO ARKANSAS** notifier. It augurs a satirical presage – **BUCKLE UP FOR SAFETY**. I hit the causeway, zigzagging to and fro, combing for my stalkers. Where are they? They've disintegrated. Shit! A patrol cruiser appears in the median, and I brake aggressively. The case ejects off the upholstery, lambasting the floorboard. I stare ahead, butterflies fluttering. Thankfully, the trooper isn't attentive, and I stream by undetected. Replacing the case, I shun the highway altogether. I'm harpooned to the veneer, powerless to avert my eyes. Holy hell. What... have... I... done?

NO CHURCH IN THE WILD

Impressions of the old-timer at The Peabody flicker through my psyche as I relive our conversation. He was unwavering in his allegation that it was me. That I was the guy who stranded this briefcase with him a year ago. Had I not known better, I would've surmised him to have been a personage of sterling integrity formulated purely on how he carried himself and confidently relayed that cockamamie anecdote. But I do know better, and he's a goddamn liar because his contentions were patently untrue. Why though? What logical explanation could there be? You don't fabricate fraudulence out of the blue. Perhaps somebody bribed him, or blackmailed him, or…

Which brings us to the goon squad. If they coveted the briefcase, why didn't they snatch it forthright? I couldn't have prevented them. Unless… Are there ancillary hints to whatever I'm wrapped up in? A semitruck blares its horn as I've inadvertently veered across the broken white lines. The menacing clang startles me from my catatonia. Must gather my wits. I'm uncertain of where I am. Everything's a blur – billboards, roadside attractions, route markers. My brain's on the brink of rupturing, with the precursory developments circulating turbulently. Just then the GPS apprises that I'm merging onto 70 East, and I change lanes. The climactic phase of this Kafkaesque caper has arrived. Peering through the windshield, I grit my teeth. The sky is a landfill. There's a sign for Effingham, Illinois, mounted above, and The Cross at the Crossroads looms yet again.

Visions of my mother and father emanate, and I can't neutralize them. I ponder my existence and the mode I've spent my days in the wake of their passing. Making them proud was all I ever wanted. Did I fulfill that objective, or would they be mortified by the adult I've matured into? Living up to their legacy is inconceivable, but I'm doing the best I can, dammit. Aren't I? They perpetually proclaimed me as a sweet boy with a bright future. I used to have a purpose.

Now look at me. I've become a vapid, materialistic, self-centered douchebag without an ounce of substance: no spouse, no children, no faith. I'm nothing. I'm less than nothing. I'm… Quit it! Drive your ass home and get to the bottom of this before you go stark raving mad. **Mental note:** ....

REVELATIONS

Fortunately, there's no trace of Darby's SUV in my driveway. I don't harbor the bandwidth to schmooze. I input the keypad password, duck underneath the garage, and bowl inside. A solitary beep echoes, insinuating she neglected to employ the sensors – shocker. I yeet the briefcase and dart for the toilet. I haven't peed in hours, and I'm gonna explode.

After I freshen up, I corral my toolbox, then plonk onto the Persian rug. Lacking the acumen to unscramble the 3-dial locking hardware, I calculate blunt force is the obvious solution. Right away, I attempt jimmying the latches – nope. Next, I wedge a screwdriver between the segments, then pummel it with a mallet. I whack my knuckle and yelp in agony. On the heels of various unsuccessful experiments utilizing a myriad of instruments and techniques, I relent. Tools decorate the tapestry while the battered carryall stays intertwined. I'm pining for a recipe to soothe the discomfort.

Hurriedly, I migrate to the kitchen and snag a tumbler and bottle of Maker's Mark off the bar cart. I pour the bourbon to the rim and swill. It's insufficient. I ransack the medicine cabinet, hunting for the antidote. The brunt of my prescriptions and over-the-counter remedies are either bare or unsuitable to accomplish the goal. At long last, I cop a jar of illegally obtained Xanax, Percocet, and Vicodin ensconced behind a vitamin canister, fish out some pills, and gulp them down with the brown liquor. I'm prepped to take a third swig when it strikes me that I never closed the garage. I reopen the door and spy outside. The drink slips from my grasp, shattering on the epoxy. I'm incapacitated. The Cadillac's quartered parallel to my rental, unoccupied.

Without so much as glancing at the shards, I backtrack and lumber toward the parlor – anguish compounding step-by-step. Timorously, I crane my neck around the dividing wall and calcify.

A thirtysomething male donning a forest green suit perches on my Corbusier armchair, legs crossed, hands steepled. The four henchmen brood at his dorsum – draped in black, as they were. Contrary to our previous interactions, they've axed their Ray-Bans, naked eyes pasted to mine. How did I not hear them? And who the fuck is…?

"Fetch me the briefcase," the clandestine leader postulates. Goose bumps jut ubiquitously. I'm rooted to the porcelain. My medulla oblongata inept at integrating the signal sent by my nervous system. "Now!" he growls malevolently, galvanizing my constitution. I dash from the entryway, clench the handle, then return. "Sit," he dictates, gesturing toward the scarlet velvet couch. I plant myself on the middle cushion and roost the shell atop the coffee table separating us.

I feel dazed and confused. "Who… Who are you?" I quiz frailly.

"I'm the spectre at the feast."

"Hmm? I don't…"

"Tsk, tsk, tsk," he intervenes, wagging an admonishing finger. "You're asking the wrong question."

My anatomy's undulating amok, head in danger of popping off my spinal column. I'm incarcerated within a delusion, a chimera, a vile figment of my imagination.

The nefarious intruder snaps impatiently, ruthlessly. "Focus," he ordains. "Why would five strangers break into your house apart from robbing you?"

Steadily, my evaluation flops to the attaché.

"Bingo. Then if it wouldn't be too much trouble."

I skid the leather across the surface.

"Stop!"

Unhesitatingly, I reinstate my erect pose.

"I want you to do it!"

"Ih-Ih-It won't budge."

"Did you enter the combination?"

"The combination? If I knew that, I'd…"

"You should, since you're the imposter who set it."

I'm befuddled. My sensibilities have tapered. "This is a huge misunderstanding. The briefcase isn't even… I scooped it up at…"

"It's unrecognizable to you?"

"No… yeah… There's this tiny town and…"

"Your father."

A lump forms in my throat. "My father? What about my father?" I oppugn leerily, reproachfully.

"It belonged to your father."

I swallow hard and regard him vacuously. Striving to deconstruct his query, I study the receptacle. Memories of my old man kissing his wife and kid goodbye, preliminary to departing for the office, whir through me like the blades of a helicopter. How could this be his? "I'm not, uh…"

"Your birthdate," he asserts. My skin draws rigid, dome contorting in dismay. He speaks lazily, overexaggerated enunciation. "Try. Your. Birthdate."

"My birth…" I dwindle, our perceptions conjoined. His obsidian irises are borderline demonic. I'm consumed by fright, skeleton paralyzed.

Gradually, his hand elevates, then forcibly motions downward. "The clock's ticking."

Although it's a seemingly straightforward mandate, my ability to recall the day I was born is in remission. My hippocampus has logged off. Must decompress. Deep breaths, deep breaths. As my heart rate slows, the wheels begin turning. Finally, it comes to me – April 3rd, 1987. I fidget with the locks, but I'm quaking.

"Ten seconds," he advises. The countdown commences, vastly proliferating my anxiousness.

I take another stab, incrementally scrolling the leftward dial: 0-4-0. I transition starboard, rotating the digits: 3-8-7. I'm jittery yet align both thumbs on the metallic squares. When he enumerates two, I push in, and the hasps disengage. I back away, relinquishing an oral sigh of alleviation.

"Attaboy," the monster jeers, offering toxic praise. "Now open it."

I'm too afraid to find out. And once I execute this directive, my usefulness to them will adjourn. However, with thoughts of impending doom churning, my frontal lobe declines to draft an evacuation plan.

"We're waiting," he admonishes.

Sketches of heroin, diamonds, cash, and guns inundate my cerebral cortex. Despair permeates with the inevitable around the corner. Sizing up my oppressors, I suck in presumably my dying breath and hoist the lid.

"Well?" he asks.

Mystification abounds. There aren't any opiates, any stones, any currency, or any weapons. Nothing but loads of Polaroids sprawled along the base. Grabbing wads, I simultaneously organize them in a manner that allows me to review, then shuffle successively. Just like the pictures from the terminal, each is a Marfan point of interest with handwritten dates glazing the margins. And just like those, plus the ones I took myself, the script matches universally.

I abstract several versions of the Prada installation to compare. They're primarily homogeneous, yet there's a principal disparity. I sift through the madness, frenetically pawing the negatives, training my gaze on the landmarks, then the chronological indicator, sans comprehension. Shots highlighting the water tower, the ballroom, the theater, and so forth, irrefutably penned by the same individual, except the numeric sequences differentiate. I forgo my investigation. "What are these?"

"Give it a minute."

My intellect has dissolved. None of this computes. Exasperation bursts at the seams, and his ambiguity is infuriating. I'm coming unhinged. "I haven't the faintest fucking notion!" I yowl viciously.

"Then reach into the front pocket."

Mimicking the antics of a petulant child, I cross my arms. My diabolical opponent watches, relishing the torment being inflicted. He's shamelessly aware he holds all the cards. If I value what lies ahead, there's no recourse short of obeying his command. I've come too far to turn back at this stage. As a consequence, I succumb.

The upper partition contains expanding accordion flaps, and I evulse a manila envelope. I unwind the cord on the string-and-button closure, then eradicate a mound of tarnished newsprint. The reports, dated December 26, 2010, were amassed from assorted Texas periodicals. I peruse them with a cursory glimpse. They pertain to a car wreck. My neural pathways collide. I can't assimilate this. Spontaneously, my dexterity energizes, and I commute to the man in green.

"Do I have your attention now?" he instigates corrosively.

Warily, I hark back to the clippings. Each incorporates images from the aftermath. Those of the wreck itself appear generally connate, but the supporting visuals vary, displaying people at the scene. *The Dallas Morning News* published a graphic of the coroner. *Austin American-Statesman* spotlights an EMT and paramedic. *Houston Chronicle* accents a police detective. And the *El Paso Times* reveals the innocent bystander who phoned in the mishap.

"Take a closer look at the photos," he demands.

"Why?"

"Because I said so!"

I heighten the Houston excerpt again. My curiosity transfixed to the officer's contours. With utmost urgency, I lunge for the Austin write-up and canvass the medics flanking their ambulance, hovering above a body bag. They seem vaguely familiar. I pounce on the El Paso summary and analyze the eyewitness. Jesus H. Christ! I've seen every single one of them. But how? From where? I'm unable to tie the recognition to a memory. Suddenly, it hits me like a ton of bricks.

ANGRY CHAIR

The surveillance of the room bores into me as I scope the men in black. It's them. They were there. Each a part of the catastrophic finale, stemming from the chain of events that claimed my parents' lives. I gawk at the harbinger of my ruin. He tilts his cranium, beckoning me toward the briefcase once more. What now?

"Dallas," he barks sinisterly.

"Dallas? I don't…" I clam up. There's a remaining feature I've yet to explore. I glove the snippet, immediately possessed by the coroner's eyes. A pair of eyes I'll reminisce about till kingdom come. I shudder and emit a terrifying, whimpering scream. Teardrops gush vehemently.

I prop my elbows on my thighs and entomb my face in my palms. I weep, hopeless to thwart it. I'm undergoing a full-blown meltdown. The coroner was the guy at the viewing platform. Why would they get rid of *him*? I hike my perspective listlessly to observe my adversary. He's sedated, icy-cold stare leveled at me. Meanwhile, the others have fled.

I kangaroo off the sofa, scouring the periphery furiously, then streak for the garage. The Mercedes endures at the tail of my Audi, but the Cadillac's absent. I race back into the den and throw down the gauntlet.

"Where the fuck are your friends?!" He abstains from replying. "Answer me, you piece of shit! Answer me!" I snarl ferociously.

"Read."

"Read what?!"

"The article."

"Fuck that! First you…"

"You're in no position to negotiate. Sit down and do as you're told," he stipulates.

I'm stationary, surveying him. He doesn't flinch. Resentfully, I charge to the table and clutch the paper.

DISASTROUS CHRISTMAS DAY TRAFFIC ACCIDENT DEATH TOLL REACHES THREE

On the outskirts of Marfa, two vehicles were involved in a head-on collision off U.S. Route 67/U.S. Route 90.

I pore over the introductory paragraph repeatedly. Marfa? This has to be a misprint.

Both passengers inside a silver Lexus IS 250, traveling toward the famed West Texas town, died as a result of being propelled from their automobile. The driver of a purple Ford Mustang, navigating in the direction of Alpine, was pronounced DOA.

I abort the examination, BPM's skyrocketing.

"It's essential you finish. Your divine awakening awaits," he edifies.

"My what?"

"Finish it!"

Reluctantly, I surrender.

According to law enforcement officials, the man and woman in the Lexus weren't wearing seat belts. The owner of the Mustang suffered fatal injuries when his airbag failed to deploy.

This makes zero sense. They wore their harnesses religiously. Dad wouldn't start the engine unless everyone was securely fastened. Even those in the rear. Mom and I heckled him unremittingly. Equally alarming – how the exposé depicts the participants. It excludes the quantity per respective machine, but plainly specifies the <u>driver</u> trekking east and the <u>passengers</u> heading west perished. Were neither of my parents driving?

A passerby alerted authorities at approximately 4:30 p.m. "I trailed a few car lengths behind the Mustang. Then, wham… it sped away like a bat out of hell," Van Horn resident Jon Sinder declared. "By the time I caught up, the damage had already been done. I slammed on the brakes and swerved off the road to avoid barreling into the wreckage."

The lone survivor is the operator of the Lexus. Paramedics rushed him to Alpine's Big Bend Regional Medical Center. Sources attest he's in critical but stable condition after being knocked unconscious and sustaining facial lacerations.

Without delay, I lurch for the complementary newspapers and vet hastily. They disseminate the identical saga and intricacies, save the names or relationships of anyone. I shred the columns, and the strips waft earthbound.

"You didn't enjoy that story?" the insidious fuck irks callously.

"WHO WAS THE DRIVER?!" I howl.

A spiteful rictus blossoms across his chops. "In due course. There's plenty yet to come."

"Why are you doing this?"

"That's the million-dollar question. So, let's see if what's behind door number two modifies your naïveté."

"I won't play this game."

"Oh, you'll do precisely that; otherwise, you'll never know."

"Know what?"

"The truth."

"The truth about what? My parents? They're fucking dead, and they aren't coming back. That's all I need to know."

"False! There's more, and this shall continue. Now stick your goddamn hand into that goddamn briefcase and remove the contents of the other pocket!"

His fangs deepen. I'm at his mercy, obligated to humor him until I decrypt this riddle. A kraft mailing pouch is burrowed within, and I draw out a sheet, folded into thirds. I unfurl, then dissect. Another *Austin American-Statesman* citation dated December 27, 2010. The header transmits **LOCAL NEWS**. I skim the captions: a shopping mall fundraiser, a holiday concert at Stubb's Waller Creek Amphitheater, a calendar of New Year's Eve soirees. Side B advertises:

REGIONAL NEWS
WEST TEXAS YULETIDE DEBACLE

I stray from the commentary and glower at the sadist. He's torpid, expecting satiation of his instructions. It's time to end this.

Authorities have released the identities for all parties involved in the horrific late afternoon fender-bender between Alpine and Marfa on Christmas Day. Gabriel Evans, 37, of Denton, was the driver of the purple Ford Mustang.

A candid headshot shows the victim during happier days. It takes a fraction of a second to descry the person in the photo is the wraith appearing before me. My flesh numbs, and I'm helpless to divert consideration. Fluid cascades onto my lap as the crying resurrects.

"Don't raise the white flag. You're almost there," he goads. My eyelids adhere, and I convulse uncontrollably. "Open your eyes," he imposes virulently, escalating my apprehension. "OPEN YOUR FUCKING EYES!" he roars, rattling the foundation. My functions ignite, still too scared to oppose the enigmatic figure who has been given a name – the name of Gabriel. Through the lacrimation, I circle back for the epilogue.

The passengers of the silver Lexus IS 250 were Richard and Beverly Kates, both 52, from Indianapolis, Indiana. Forensic specialists established the couple's son, Brady, was operating the vehicle. He's in intensive care at Alpine's Big Bend Regional Medical Center. The cause of the crash remains unresolved.

A photo of us celebrating my folks' 25th wedding anniversary exhibited below the text. Flatline…

"How dreadful wisdom can be when it yields a ghastly revelation to the blind. Wouldn't you agree, *Brady*?" Gabriel solicits brashly.

They say a picture is worth a thousand words, but as I goggle at the portrait of my family, I perceive one word exclusively a thousand times over – KILLER. I venture to register the sum total of what I've just gleaned. And yet, with this preponderance of evidence in front of me, I'm simply unequipped to cite any of it actually occurring. Roughly a decade since the accident and not a certifiable anamnesis.

"How'd it happen?" I ask pitifully.

"You tell me. I'm entitled to your confession."

"Forgive me. I am so, so…"

"An apology?! Meaningless. He's reserved repentance for the righteous."

"How can I fix this with you?"

"The only thing you owe me is… everything!"

My motor skills are inoperable. "I-I-I…c-c-c…"

"Remember."

"But… But how?"

"That's your call. We've reprised this performance, year after year."

"Huh?"

He glares incredulously. "Who's responsible for those Polaroids? Who hid that key? Who clipped the bulletins?"

"I have no idea."

His stranglehold on the chair tightens, and the erewhile pitch-black orbs brim with molten lava as the inner volcano gets ready to erupt. Gabriel distends his arm, fist balled in rage, forefinger extended to label the guilty. The quietude abates, and the vitriol unleashes. "You! This is your handiwork!" he blazes cataclysmically.

My chest heaves. "That's impossible."

"Humph."

"You're not real. It's a dream. I'll wake up and you'll…"

"Enough! Last chance, so listen closely. In order to be absolved, to be purged, to be liberated from your contrition, you must bear the burden. Arise out of this stupor and forego burying the facts." He leans forward. "Inside that briefcase, there's one final clue. It rests upon your shoulders henceforth."

I swoop in posthaste, picking up Polaroids and hurling them haphazardly. I maraud both pockets, lest I've missed anything. I grope every nook and cranny for covert compartments. I sway to Gabriel – he's vanished. I soar off the furniture, pendulating in a frenzied capacity.

"Gabriel! The briefcase is empty!" I boost it toward the ozone, then bash it against the ground. It bounces and sails through the sky. My appendages fall limp, and I plummet onto the couch, lobotomized.

WAY DOWN WE GO

I've lost myself in the rosebud textured ceiling pattern. Upon acquiring this house, the builders asked which kind of brush design should be applied. Without an inkling of what they meant, I checked into my options and interrupted them as apparitions of Orson Welles doused my subliminal. Hearing Charles Foster Kane mumble the moniker of his childhood sled was all it required to arrive at such an insignificant decision. *That* I'm capable of retaining, yet my parents decease eludes me. How pathetic am I?

I loosen my immersion and perk up, coveting intel. Pinwheeling around the perimeter, I'm immobilized by an unknown object reclining adjacent from the step down linking the kitchen to the sunken bonus room. I wriggle past the documentation before hunching over for appraisal. It's the intestinal shelving of the briefcase. Must've detached when it trampolined off the flooring. I purl frantically, probing for the vessel. It's protruding behind where Gabriel eviscerated my soul, both halves split into an inverted V-shape. I kick it upright, unmasking a bulky packet taped within. I unhitch it and flump onto Satan's throne to assess.

I extricate a file folder. The color-coded tabs resemble medical records. I thumb across page after page, scanning the clinical history. Dafuq? They are *my* medical records. I suspend on longhand remarks authored by a Dr. Perry Schall, dated January 12, 2011 – shy of a month post-catastrophe.

I've conducted a host of clinical interviews, including the Structured Clinical Interview for Dissociation (SCID–D). Initial diagnosis: patient afflicted with dissociative amnesia.

Onset triggered by the car accident wherein his parents were killed. Disorder manufactured as a coping mechanism originating from extreme emotional stress and remorse. He cannot discern particulars endemic to the state of affairs surrounding the incident. Trials for dissociative identity disorder proved inconclusive, though possibility of identity loss and creation of separate identities exists. Treatment recommendations entail CBT (cognitive behavioral therapy), hypnosis, and/or drug-facilitated interview. Prognosis TBD.

Dissociative amnesia? I wonder how often and by how many experts this tidbit has been unveiled. But what's this *Fight Club* nonsense? Am I Tyler Durden? First rule of dissociative amnesia is you do not talk about dissociative amnesia. Second rule of...

I riffle through and browse auxiliary comments scribbled by a substitute psychiatrist. A Dr. Lynn T. Coy revised the dossier, January 23, 2012.

Diagnosis amended to include subtype dissociative fugue. Patient participated in an act of nomadic travel without recollection.

> After administering drug-facilitated interview, results suggest subject also incurring unique form of dissociative identity disorder. Rather than creating multiple personalities, he seems to be channeling notable parties connected with the tragedy.

The room starts spinning. Dr. Coy has unwittingly dispatched the coup de grâce. My nape sags onto the rail of the Corbusier, and the folder topples. The downward spiral is complete. Contemplations of suicide submerge my encephalon like a tsunami. Any method I can envision humans exterminating themselves flit one by one.

I labor to stand, then accumulate the elements that daub the area. I chuck them into the satchel of abominable verity and take a parting gander, scoffing cynically. I close the lid, clamp the hasps, then snare the handle. Traipsing across the kitchen, I pluck the bourbon and wend toward the bedroom. I clamber above the California King, dunk the case beside me, and unscrew the cap, slugging straight from the bottle. I'm physically and mentally bankrupt. Crawling under the linens, my body innately curves into the fetal position as I prepare for the sandman to make his grand entrance and steward me along Elm Street, permanently concluding this nightmare.

CODA

There's a guise of pure delight on my mom. She glances at me, then her husband, before twisting to behold the scenery. From the rear, he's flailing aimlessly, aspiring to consummate the most rudimentary of tasks. Profuse turmoil balloons behind his conventionally halcyon visage. The commotion augments, and the air inside the automobile grows tense.

"What's the problem?" she submits crossly.

"I can't fasten this damn thing," he whines, aggravation flaring up as he grapples with the bindings. "Son, please stop the vehicle."

"Good heavens, Richard, let me help you," she volunteers, unlatching herself from restraint.

I arch the rearview mirror, bringing Dad into the frame. He meets my scrutiny with ardent vexation, then shifts to his wife. "Beverly, get back in your seat this instant!" he fumes and clasps her wrists.

"Guys, knock it off!" I plead in desperation.

As they scuffle, she loses her balance and bangs into my deltoid. My hand jerks toward the opposite lane, impelling me to branch over the centerline. The oncoming muscle car zooms forward so hellaciously it's futile for the motorist to endeavor moving out of harm's way. He ploughs into us with pulverizing brutality. The impact hurtles my mother through the front windshield. My father catapults end to end, violently blasting out a side window. The Lexus somersaults continuously until drawing to cessation, roof atop asphalt. It seesaws for a spell, eventually coming to a standstill in the middle of the highway, debris scattered everywhere.

IN THE BARDO

I'm roused by a silky, feminine croon. "C'mon, sleepyhead. Rise and shine," she coaxes, tenderly fondling my sleeve.

"Mom?" I gurgle.

"Ew. Are you alright?" Darby needles.

I recalibrate my pupils and grunt, "Not in the least."

She scurries to the faucet, then rushes back. "Drink this," she exhorts, dispensing a mug and bolstering me against the headboard. "When did you get home? We haven't spoken for days. What gives?"

"I've been a little preoccupied."

"You look like shit," she broadcasts blithely before segueing to the bane of my existence. "Dare I ask?" I shirk her inquest. "Okey doke, I'll take the bait. What's in the briefcase, Brady?"

"My life," I rasp bitterly, setting down the mug, then winging aside the bedspread en route to the bathroom. I splash cold water on my skin, yank the washcloth off the rack, and swab. Lowering it lackadaisically, my eyes peek over the fabric. I seethe with fury at the duplicitous facsimile. Diffidently, I stroke my scar.

"So, how was your precious Marfa?" she jabs from a distance.

I pelt the rag at my doppelgänger, then reenter. "None of your business," I bluster.

"Well, you're in a splendid mood. Would you prefer I pack my bags?"

We're mute as she shoots daggers at me. There's no excuse for acting malevolently. She isn't to blame, and despite my self-loathing, I could use the companionship. I thrust her backward coltishly and snuggle up. "I'm an asshole."

"What's your glitch? You don't seem normal."

"That's the understatement of the century, chica." I haul the attaché onto my legs and unlock. She peers at the materials, and the peaceful demeanor abruptly abolishes. Darby rifles through the photos, uprears the shredded newspaper articles, then notices the portfolio.

"What is all this?"

"My schizophrenic scrapbook."

"But the Polaroids… Why do they…?" Her diction palls.

"Gimme that," I implore, nodding at the Maker's.

"A wee early for whiskey, Hemingway." I sulk. "I'm just sayin'," she taunts, nabs the bottle, and passes it. I uncap the top, quaff, then pass it back. She stares at me, radiating that 'you're insane' expression. "Fuck it!" she exclaims, pounding a shot of her own.

I dislodge the bottle from her, then have an additional nip, deliberating how to proceed. "Darby… I was driving when my parents died." Inchmeal, I corkscrew toward her. She's trembling.

"I know," she utters meekly.

My brow creases. "Pardon me?"

She bites her lip. "You've told me."

"What in God's name are you blathering about?" She doesn't respond. "Say it." Her reticence prolongs. "Just fucking tell me!" I shout, and she covers herself. My temper promptly counteracted by disgrace. I compose myself, then hug her. "I'm sorry for raising my voice, but you're my only hope."

"You sure you wanna travel down this road?"

"Hundred percent."

We're nonverbal while she inspects me. Darby inhales strongly, then exhales sharply. "Here goes… A nurse rang after you were admitted at the hospital. He…"

"How?"

"How what?"

"How did that nurse get your number?"

"I'm listed as your emergency contact. Now shut your stinking mouth and pay attention."

"Copy that."

She glouts, then resumes. "He supplied status updates but wouldn't speculate further. The second we hung up I went berserk, threw clothes into a duffel, and taxied to the airport. I slept in the lobby because there weren't any flights available remotely near Marfa.

"The next morning, I boarded the first plane, then bussed an extra 200 miles. Upon arrival, they'd upgraded you from critical to fair, and your vital signs improved drastically. They had you so heavily medicated you floated in and out of consciousness. Your face was bruised, forehead bandaged, and I sat by your side, bawling. When you revived, I practically mauled you. The staff barged in, ran a slew of tests, then you chatted with the doctors. Once everybody deserted, we watched TV and ate that disgusting cafeteria food. Hours elapsed until you spilled your guts and…" She becomes uncharacteristically taciturn.

"And? What'd I disclose?" She pivots toward the wall. I graze her chin, gently guiding her back. "No matter how unpleasant it is, you can't protect me."

"Please, I…"

"Darby, I'm begging you."

She hesitates, soughs, then concedes. "The three of you were headed to Marfa, and less than thirty miles from the hotel, your father pulled into a convenience store to relieve himself. In typical Kates family fashion, you and your mother ganged up on the guy. Thought it was hilarious he couldn't hold it. Anyway, he exited, you leapt in front, he came back, and you refused to move, so he hopped behind.

"Apparently, he had issues with his belt and got upset. Your mom became pissy and whirled around to assist. Then they yelled at each other, and you urged them to stop, but…" She tarries, monitoring me.

"But?"

"You were hazy on the specifics. Basically, he sorta shoved her, and instead of landing in her seat, she bumped into your shoulder, causing you to lose control."

"And then?"

"There's no and then. That's everything you indicated at the hospital and everything you've indicated since."

"Since? Since what?"

"*This*," she screeches, waving her arm in a semi-circular motion. "This recurring narrative. You leave, you reappear, then regurgitate the details you're competent of."

"I don't recall us ever discussing this."

"Welp, it's an annual tradition. When it originally initiated, I dove down a rabbit hole researching the depths of memory loss, and some of the examples were bananas."

"Elaborate."

"Individuals randomly sunbathing at the beach, then forgetting how they surfaced. Others cultivated new lives entirely. There's a thesis on a software engineer who emigrated from San Francisco to Phoenix, assumed a brand-new persona, bought a brand-new wardrobe, began a brand-new job, etcetera, etcetera. Months later, he awoke without retention of doing so."

"Thrilling," I spiel perplexedly. "How's this relevant?"

She blinks, uncommunicative, excessively distraught. "Your yearly road trip… You always go to Marfa."

I scowl at her, baffled by the assertion. "The hell you say! That isn't true."

"Yes, it is."

"Evidently, I went with Rick and Bev a decade prior, but I haven't gone back 'til this past weekend."

"Oh yeah? Where'd you go last year?" She leers at me, and I toil to summon the location. Darby's inflection aggrandizes as the grilling perseveres. "Where'd you go two years ago? Where'd you go five years ago? Where'd you go…?"

"Cut it out!"

"These are simple questions."

"Wait a minute, goddammit!" I rummage the deepest recesses of my mind. They're blank.

"Ain't ringin' any bells?"

"I can't remember. Why the fuck can't I remember?"

"Because your brain won't let you."

"Lay off the psychobabble bullshit!"

"It's legit, B. Something's rejecting your preservation of those flashbacks."

"I don't believe you."

"I'm not making this crap up, dildo."

"Then why haven't you divulged anything previously?"

"I have! The November following the accident, you'd sorted the logistics for your excursion, and I attempted to tag along. I didn't think you should be alone given the circumstances. You shrugged it off and behaved super shady. Even kept your destination a massive secret until I gave you the third degree, and… You replied with Marfa. I just stood there, speechless. I couldn't fathom why you'd possibly consider that after what occurred. But before I pressed you, shit turned weird."

"Weird how?"

"You droned on and on about having dreamed of visiting yet hadn't. Then you spewed a boatload of stuff you'd read regarding the town, and that's the moment I realized… You were truly oblivious."

"And did you convey these relatively substantial findings?"

"No, I was stunned. Then I figured, if he sees this through, things could potentially click, and the memories might come flooding back. And in the beginning, that's the way it unfolded. As soon as you returned, you broke down. Like your brain flipped a switch and started functioning properly. But shortly thereafter, you relapsed."

"What about the pictures? Have I ever shown you the pictures?"

"Not once, I swear."

"What about Gabriel or the dudes that chased me or the man in the field?"

"Who? You're scaring me."

"The driver of the vehicle I struck and everyone at the site. I've never mentioned them?"

"Never. You just recount as many of the generalities as you can. It's invariably the same convo every time."

I curtail our exchange and drift into space. Supposing these proclamations are somehow factual, why hasn't she viewed the Polaroids? And why haven't we discussed Gabriel or the paramedics or the cop or... the crusade at the lighting platform that incited this charade? Is it all hallucinatory? How screwed up am I? I'm unable to compartmentalize what's valid and what isn't and what's transpired and what didn't. The suicidal tendencies reemerge and seize custody of my desecrated equilibrium.

"Darby, I can't do this anymore."

"Agreed, it's getting far too intense. Let's hit pause," she counsels, massaging my neck. "We'll..."

"You don't understand. I can't... carry on living."

She heeds me stoically. With cheeks flush, she jacks her palm skyward, then smacks me across the jaw.

"OW! What was that for?"

"How dare you!"

"Have you not heard a word I've just said? I killed my parents! It's *my* fucking fault."

"It's not your fault! It's not your fault whatsoever. Have you not heard a word *I've* just said?!"

"Huh?"

"It was an accident, Brady. Your dad shoved your mom, and she rammed into you."

"But I…"

"But nothing. You want more proof? The police, the investigators, the insurance adjusters independently reached corresponding verdicts. I'm shocked those testimonials aren't inside that case of yours."

"How could they?"

"The exact legalese escapes me. Something about comparative, um… negluh… neglih… comparative negligence. That's it."

"Explain."

"Texas is a tort state, implying the courts deduce who's liable. In your scenario, Mr. Mustang's madcap speeding constituted the singular demonstrable item. And seeing as you weren't seeking financial restitution in conjunction with him not having next of kin to cause a stir, the whole kit and caboodle got swept under the rug."

"And that makes things right?"

"Most certainly doesn't."

"Then what does it mean?"

"It means there was fuck-all you could've done to prevent the collision, and you're lucky to be breathing," she argues.

My world is upside down and sideways. Staying alive seems pointless, and I'm skeptical of how much longer I can tolerate it. Contrastingly, I cannot hurt another person, particularly one who fancies me unconditionally. I commend what Darby's essaying to achieve, but she's contributed bupkis that carries weight. Congratulations, shithead! You didn't receive a jail sentence after killing your parents. As a consolation, you'll stomach that knowledge for eternity.

That's nugatory. Ending my life won't expedite a reunion. They're somewhere high above, and I'm on the road to perdition. At any rate, haven't I dishonored them enough? They deserve better.

"I just… I'm clueless how to move forward," I fess up ruefully.

"Begin by promising me you'll never speak that way again, you selfish prick."

I snort at her candor. She cries, and I merely watch. I'm unworthy of her commiseration. I strain for a napkin on the nightstand and dab her tears. "I promise." Defusing the quarrel is the appropriate course of action, irrespective of my subsequent intentions.

"I'll murder you myself before allowing you to commit suicide, stupid idiot!" We share an artificial laugh.

"Truthfully though, I'm at the end of my rope."

"You need help, babe. You ditched the psychiatrists and meds years ago."

"Whatever's necessary. Will you help? Will you help me repair this?"

"Are you kidding? We're in this together."

I huff fervidly, musing over my strategy. It's unfair to place this solely on her, but who else can I appeal to? I ascend, glom my cell off the dresser, and dial. Darby noses toward the foot of the bed.

"What's up, Doc? It's Brady Kates. Thanks for taking my call." I pace the carpeting as we converse. "Wouldn't bother you if there wasn't a crisis. Could you see me this afternoon? It's important." She reviews her schedule. "One sec." I cup the mouthpiece. "Would you accompany me to my therapy appointment at 3:00 p.m.?" I ask Darby.

"Absolutely."

I crouch to kiss her temple, then confer with Julie. She accedes contingent upon our signing a consent form. "No problema. Ciao." I lob the phone onto the duvet, fatigued.

Darby rises, bevels into me, and squeezes tenaciously.

PAINT IT BLACK

As we enter the office, I acquaint the ladies. Julie ushers us toward the chaise, then delivers the release. We autograph the paperwork, and the session commences.

"Something big must've happened to compel the outreach," my therapist avows, presiding from her chair.

"You could say that."

"Begin with Darby. Since launching our partnership, you've never invited anyone to sit in. Why now?"

I'm closemouthed auditing her. Although this meeting was my idea, I'm justifiably hesitant to talk. Today's different. Entertaining the shrink isn't my aspiration. I'm here to mend, or at minimum, start the process. I steer toward my sidekick. She gleams a reassuring countenance, imparting that everything will be fine. Darby's a candle in the darkness of my mortal coil. I snicker, communicating I'm appreciative, then revert to Julie, ready to come clean.

"The short answer – she's stuck by me through thick and thin."

"But why has it taken this long?"

"The thing is… I don't know the proper vernacular to articulate this effectively, so I'll phrase it in language I relate to and hopefully it'll become transparent. Cool?"

"Cool."

I inspire. "You're both terribly mindful of my nerdy obsession with movies. Well, there's this, uh, unwritten policy necessitating most plotlines revolve around the theme of good versus evil. Where the hero defeats the villain, and the story ends happily ever after." I stall a beat. "Turns out that in my biopic, the protagonist and antagonist are unexpectedly reciprocal. And neither wins, and this drama repeats itself again and again and again." The women fixate on me, slightly disturbed, but it's imperative I hear it and accept it, once and for all. "Accidentally or not, I'm accountable for the death of my parents.

"My friend here has known for quite a while. And, if I had to hazard a guess, I'd suspect you did, as well. Would my intuition be accurate?" To the surprise of nobody, Julie bobs in the affirmative. "Lovely. Then we're on the same page. So, before I forfeit ownership of this newfound wealth of information, I reckoned confronting it might prove wise. Imagined us three could brainstorm and carve out a blueprint forging ahead. Because I'd sooner die than reconvene next year, reliving this for the umpteenth time. I'm ignorant of what I or we have..." I snivel. "This needs to stop, and it won't without your guidance and reinforcement."

Darby rubs my leg. Julie extends a box of Kleenex and lauds, "I'm elated you're inclined to put forth the effort. It's undeniably a step in the right direction. Yet I'd be remiss if I forsook advising you there isn't an actual cure. No magic pill you swallow and make the maladies disappear."

"Duly noted."

"Okay, let's dive right in then. You've probably ascertained that you're plagued by multiple disorders deriving from the ordeal. First, there's the amnesia facet. Pretty standard in instances as traumatic as yours. Oftentimes, the patient responds favorably to treatment and salvages expunged remembrances, contemporaneously learning to cope with the grief.

"On top of this, you suffer from an ailment titled dissociative fugue. In a nutshell, those affected can perform acts, ordinarily involving travel of some kind, grasping full cognizance as it materializes. When the fugue state expires, they're incapable of dredging up the aforenamed undertakings. It's a rare syndrome estimated to develop in fewer than two-tenths of a percent of the populace. The optimistic outlook is, over the passage of time, you'll maintain the memory, and the fugue, represented by your perennial voyage to Marfa, dissipates."

Darby clocks me, flabbergasted, and I requite the reaction.

"Safe to presume we've covered this?" I cross-examine.

"Yes, usually amid our inaugural gathering post-resurgence. We broach the topic, and you seem to connect the dots, then the retrospections progressively diminish until you've forgotten altogether. And out of sensitivity for your wishes and my personal and professional code of ethics, I've never pushed. I proffered subtle intimations or gestures, but if ever you felt distressed, I backed off straightaway."

"How do I conquer this?" I poll as though a chemist synthesized a vaccine for a decennium of mental instabilities.

"Unfortunately, there's no definitive resolution. Square one — persistent discussion. Your willingness to contest it is an excellent stepping stone. That said, it'll merit tons of hard work. In addition, we could revisit the psychotherapy and pharmaceuticals. Purely a question of the lengths you're prepared to go."

Darby sheepishly raises her hand. "May I?" she targets at Julie.

"Please."

Darby looks to me for permission, and I assent. "Brady and I have canvassed this ad nauseam, and it's just as you've described. He comes home, rehashes the nitty-gritty, then it deletes. I've tried every technique imaginable. Nothing has succeeded. Perhaps you could offer some pointers. Odds are we'll be joined at the hip, so I'm hoping you'd instruct me on a daily approach."

"Well, Brady's made a real breakthrough. He's routinely expressed an ambivalence toward addressing his folks by reason of the situation, in his words, being 'too painful' and that it 'wouldn't change jack shit.' The disorder colluded with his apathy, and they bonded to sculpt an alliance, caching the data. Now that he's abreast of the nuances, it's crucial he remains sentient to dodge repression and lapse into the dissociative amnesia component. Therefore, I don't deem it mandatory to ventilate the subject seven days a week, but it's obviously advantageous to inject into the dialogue at intervals to substantiate amelioration."

"And the whole driving to Marfa element? Will that vaporize or simply replicate the ensuing winter?"

"There's no guarantee. On the positive side, we've exposed his impetus. Unlike the majority, Brady's fugue restricts to the chronology encircling the accident. Our best bet – focusing him as the holiday season nears to certify he doesn't experience a setback. If he stumbles, we'll devise an alternate game plan." Julie diverges her observation to me. "You're dealing with numerous complex, psychological conditions. You must take things slow and not expect an overnight transformation. Assuming you exert yourself, it's plausible you'll squelch this."

The promulgation hangs forevermore. Fuck… my… life…

"Are we having fun, yet?" Julie explores.

"So much fun," I mock.

"Smile, the heavy lifting's done, and there's still time to discuss your adventure."

I debate tackling my recent encounters with The Four Horsemen of the Apocalypse and Gabriel Evans but opt against, especially while Darby's in attendance. That girl's been through the wringer, and delving into this segment of my psychosis isn't ideal. Plus, it's hugely disconcerting Julie didn't reference them. Have I never revealed their identities to her either? Stay tuned for the next episode of *How Crazy is Brady Kates?* to unravel the mystery.

By the same token, I haven't come to terms with mutating into an older, albeit enormously better-looking Haley Joel Osment. Not only do I see dead people, but living ones who aren't actually there. Lastly, there's the teensy dilemma of my earlier self-annihilation cogitation. Opening a spare can of worms might provoke a 5150 imprisonment a la Britney. Smarter to revamp the somber atmosphere at this juncture. We could indisputably use a breather. Besides, there's an issue of quantum magnitude to untangle.

"I've got a bone to pick with you," I warn Julie.

"Pray tell."

"How many cameras have you manipulated me into purchasing?"

"HA! One per year for the preceding eight or nine years. Lord knows where they're stockpiled."

"Spill the beans. You drummed up this harebrained scheme after 'Hey Ya!' became popular."

"Erroneous. And Mr. Benjamin continues to be incorrect about shaking the negative."

"What was the genesis then?"

"A colleague endorsement. He caught wind of the practice at a seminar and instituted it on a patient. Vouched it greatly aided in jogging their memory."

"Did we ever critique the photos?"

"Incidentally, no. Whenever you'd illustrate bits and pieces concerning the exploit, you would also decree that you took Polaroids during your expedition. Thus, I interpreted it facilitating the advancement. But you've never brought any of them into our sessions. It's perdured as a source of tremendous disappointment."

"Good news, there's an overflowing briefcase at my crib if you're interested."

"Indubitably. And knock on wood, you won't recreate this in 2021, so you don't shop for another camera."

"Yeah, that ain't happening. I'm entrusting Darby with the 2020 model to remind me provided I fall off the wagon. And maybe we'll utilize it by taking a trip someplace." I swirl toward Darby. "Someplace Delta flies to."

WONDERWALL

Darby shepherds me toward the master bedroom, and I slither under the Egyptian cotton, bleary. To my astonishment, Ms. Congeniality doffs her clothing, minus the skivvies, then penetrates.

"Ahem," I mutter suspiciously.

"There's not a snowball's chance in hell I'm leaving you unchaperoned. You whined how tired you were, so we'll nap. And after the nap, we'll get hammered and then… the world is our oyster," she trumpets, winking.

Before I can react, she spins away and slopes into me, dragging my arm across her waist to secure position. I snuff deeply and soak up her essence. Those lengthy, chocolate tresses, projecting immaculately layered caramel ribbons, and fragrant tones of jasmine revitalize my moxie. I retract a couple strands, then nibble on her ear. She rolls over, and now we lie face-to-face.

We're both silent. I draw her close and caress her lips. Darby has incredible lips. Those luscious, Kim Basinger-esque lips many females crave, yet few inherently possess. What begins as a friendly peck accelerates quickly. She tugs me above her, and we partake in another sensual embrace, then disrobe.

While we make love, I gaze into her eyes. I can't recollect when I last had sex with a woman I genuinely cared about. Upon climax, I collapse onto the mattress and stare at the ceiling, respiring. I rotate toward her, and she's simpering amorously. Darby reads me like a book, anticipating my next move.

"Did you…?"

"Duh!" she proclaims. "Did you?"

"Nah, I faked." She giggles and punches me faintly.

"We could've been doing that for years, moron."

"You haven't heard? I've got this condition, and I forget stuff."

"Yeah, yeah, yeah," she says, smirking, then grabs a pillow and smothers my head briefly. She slings it onto the floor, dips between my thighs, and the second-round bell dings raucously.

I WANNA BE ADORED

As my eyelids elevate, I acquire Darby's vamoosed. Yawn. However long I've been asleep, I'm thoroughly invigorated. And no dreams, which furnishes encouragement. So, if you wouldn't mind. Allow me to reintroduce myself.

My name is Brady, and I'm not an alcoholic. I sheerly portrayed one on vacay. What's that inspirational quote? Today is the first day of the rest of your... Fuck that shit. I don't buy into such rubbish. Nevertheless, it's a golden opportunity to give the middle finger to my old life and figure out where this rerouted path lures me. Perhaps you'll follow my journey in the sequel – *Marfa Lights 2: Electric Boogaloo.* Franchise, bitch!

Footsteps leading to the room are audible. I realign, and the door creeps ajar. Darby enters, lugging a serving tray.

"Hallelujah! He has risen," she evangelizes, strapping the miniature table with legs around my lap. She's neatly arranged crockery, flatware, and condiments, and the spread smells fantastic. "Made your favorites. Cheesy scrambled eggs, corned beef hash, English muffin, grape jelly, and pulpless orange juice. Snagged a Gingerbread Latte from Starbucks, and there's some pepper and Tabasco, to boot."

"Wow, this is impressive. I didn't know you could push down the lever on a toaster, much less cook an entire meal," I enlighten cheekily as she slinks in.

"I can do lots of things you don't know, big boy," she quips, exuding a scandalous grin.

"Floozy," I sass, then rip into the chow. I've eaten zip-a-dee-doo-dah posterior to the Buc-ee's barbecue, and I'm ravenous. "When did I doze off?"

"Halfway through that Mickey Rourke thriller you worship. I glanced over, and you were comatose."

"What'd you think of the film?"

"Epic! And he was outrageously hot back in the day."

"Greatest actor of his generation and coolest motherfucker on the planet – James Dean, Steve McQueen, and a young Martin Sheen combined," I educate between munches. "Darby, this is magnificent."

"I'm happy you're happy," she avers as I chomp away. "Listen, I spoke to my mother this morning and… She'd like you to grace us with your presence at Christmas Eve dinner."

I wince and plunk the fork. "Why would you ask me that? You of all people."

"Because it's time to start fresh and put this behind you."

I sigh. "I'm nervous about…"

"About what? Eating and drinking, and playing Scrabble and Uno with my family? We aren't attending midnight mass for Chrissake. It's a glorified house party."

"Can't we chill here instead?"

"Nope. You're coming. End of story. And I'll make it worth your while."

"Hmm. I'm intrigued. What're you proposing?" I probe whimsically.

"We'll fuck in my parents' basement once they hit the sack. Do we have ourselves a deal?"

I blush. "Uh, sounds decent, I suppose."

"Hooray!" she screams, pressing her kisser against mine. "And just so we're clear, Jesus didn't kill your mom and dad, you did," she pauses, deadpan. "Too soon?"

"OH MY GOD!" I blurt in my finest Ignatius J. Reilly impersonation. No other human commands the ingenuity to conceive that type of pronouncement, let alone the gall to assert it aloud. She's truly a unicorn. "Check and mate," I declare. Darby beams widely, removes the tray, then climbs aboard. Choo choo.

SWEET OBLIVION

Before paying tribute to the man, the myth, the legend, the one and only, Almighty Messiah, I pester Darby into trailing me so I can return the rental. I fully apprehend sewing up this transaction on the 24th of December connotes the dealership will be closed. It's unquestionably a big-time cop-out snubbing Zoe. Nonetheless, 'tis a noble gesture. Furthermore, she seems like a sweet girl with a bright future ahead. Whoa, I'm totally becoming my parents.

In any event, there's zero justification for mingling. I'm not claiming it would lead anywhere, but it's illogical to even pursue. Don't get it twisted. I'm a terrific catch if the definition of "terrific" signifies a comprehensively fucked up, recovering amnesiac who shall spend the remainder of his days atoning for the deaths of three, two of whom bred him.

Bottom line: I'm too old for this shit. I told Julie I sought to settle down with somebody. Appears I've found that person directly under my nose. We might have a real shot together, and I can't afford to waste it.

I access the lot and vacate the Benz. "Fare thee well, my trusty steed," I bid the German, synchronously patting the roof. "You delivered me home unscathed. Danke schön." I slog to the building and deposit the key into the dropbox. Doubling back, I cast my inspection toward the visitor section and halt dead in my tracks. Jake's clunker hasn't left. Yikes. I appraise it from afar and cringe, then deviate to Darby. She scrunches her skin and lifts her mitts. I titter and stroll onward. Whoops, poor Jake. Bummer.

"What was that about?" she asks.

"Inside joke," I counter, jumping into the passenger seat.

"Ready to rock?"

"Aye, captain."

"Buckle up."

"Cute," I retort, complying with her requirement. "When's dinner?"

"Mom said 6:00 p.m."

"Can we make a pit stop?"

"Of course. Where we going?" Darby inquires cheerfully.

"Crown Hill," I reply, and her felicity dissolves. She eyeballs me, then sets her sights on the street and departs.

A posthumous Elliott Smith ballad streams softly in the background. I squint out the window at the Gothic Chapel, lurking abaft. Darby pilots her SUV through the cemetery gates, and I guide her toward the plot.

"This is it," I announce, and she decelerates.

"Want me to come?"

"I should handle this on my own."

"I'll wait here."

I nuzzle her, then slip outside. Meandering along the row, oscillating languorously, I'm having difficulty recalling their precise burial placement. To be frank, it's been a minute since I visited. Pending a hasty search, I find what I'm looking for.

Towering in front of the companion gravestone, six feet atop their eternal resting spot, a glimmer of daylight shines upon me. I see my shadow across the grass and leer, thinking how badly I'd relish burning it away. Prior to that, I'm obliged to reconcile the reality it's the part of me culpable for my transgressions. Whilst ashamed of those bygone sins, they embody who I am heretofore. Yet there's no moving forward without banishing that very shame, and I'm finally qualified to face my demons.

BEVERLY ANNE KATES
JUNE 9, 1962 – DECEMBER 25, 2010
LOVING WIFE AND MOTHER

RICHARD MICHAEL KATES
NOVEMBER 3, 1962 – DECEMBER 25, 2010
LOVING HUSBAND AND FATHER

I gape yearningly at the engravings and crumble to the earth, weeping. "I miss you both so goddamn much. I promise I'll turn over a new leaf. I promise I'll reform my ways. I promise I'll…" I wane, staring at the epitaph. A hand grips my clavicle, and I uncover Darby, sobbing. I cling to her, draining the emotion within, as she weaves her fingers through my hair.

WHITE XMAS

"Just relax, my mom and dad adore you," Darby comforts, pulling into the driveway. "Tonight's gonna be wonderful." She slides over and smooches me. Exiting the vehicle, it starts snowing. How fucking cliché.

"Ho ho ho, ya filthy animal," Darby larks.

"Pretty, pretty, pretty good," I Larry.

Her parents greet us on the porch. I'm confident she's briefed them. Doesn't matter. For all intents and purposes, they're the closest thing to relatives I've got at this point. I present a bottle of cheap red wine, and they escort us indoors. Let the record show, these were the last grapes standing after Darby's carnage.

The ladies defect to the kitchen, and her father squires me into the study.

"You a bourbon man, Brady?" he interrogates, eyebrows arched.

"Indeed, I am, sir."

"Perfect. I've been saving this Pappy 20 for eons. I'd say it's high time we emancipate the geezer."

"Um, yes, please," I respond, giddy at the prospect. He's referring to the brand Pappy Van Winkle, and this is from their personal reserve, barreled two decades. It resides amongst the rarest of its class. Shit costs five stacks on the secondary market. Baller.

He swipes a couple of snifters, plops in a gigantic ice block, and pours freely. "I know better than to wish you a Merry Christmas, so I shan't," he jests, handing me the beverage.

"I appreciate that."

He hoists his glass and proceeds with a toast. "To health, wealth, and happiness."

"Amen." We clink, then sip. Blimey, it's flawless – flavors of toffee, vanilla, cinnamon, oak, and citrus, plus a hint of fine leather. We slump into the matching Eames loungers, and he flips through the channels on the flat screen.

I swivel toward Darby. She peeks at me and flashes an exceedingly coquettish smile. We ogle one another interminably. Damn, she's beautiful. And her love for me is apparent. I'll do everything in my power to make this successful. I fear the friendship deteriorating if the romance fizzles, but I need her currently more than I've ever needed anybody.

Gunfire redirects my attention. Her dad has chosen *Die Hard.* "Yippee Ki Yay, Mother Trucker!" Bruce, in tandem with an incompatible dubbed voice, bellows. It's network television, for Pete's sake.

"Solid movie," he contends.

"The best!" I extol.

"C'mon boys, supper's served," our hostess spouts gleefully, schlepping a large pot of roasted chicken into the dining area.

Her father grimaces due to the fact we won't witness Hans Gruber plunging to his demise. I nod as a sign of brotherhood before relocating, bourbons in tow. He sits at the head, and I squat opposite. The women put the finishing touches on the place settings, then join at our sides. We pass trays of mashed potatoes, stuffing, and steamed vegetables, cramming our plates, which is customary for the season. The banquet gets underway, and the four of us engage in a variety of topics. Her folks are extraordinary individuals, reminiscent of mine. Darby was correct, per usual. This doesn't feel like the holiday being forced down my throat whatsoever. And I must admit, I'm legitimately enjoying it.

The feast concludes, and they declutter the dishware, then trot out an assortment of desserts and coffee. Darby's mom and dad distribute embarrassing stories from her youth. She playfully retaliates with ludicrous tales at their expense. We loaf around chuckling, basking in each other's company, and I'm overwhelmed by a true state of bliss. *This* is family. A concept I haven't understood for ages.

"I cannot express how grateful I am for the invitation," I profess, tears forming delicately in the corners of my eyes. Darby compassionately pinches my kneecap below the tablecloth.

"We're delighted to have you, dear. You're always welcome here," her mother clarifies affectionately.

"That means a lot. And your daughter fibbed. You're a spectacular chef," I clown.

"Oh, that's rich, Brady," she relays mirthfully.

"If you'll excuse me." As I spring up, Darby cuffs my wrist.

"You okay?" she sweats.

"Beyond imagination." I bow and whisper in her ear, "Thank you."

I plod into the bathroom and outstretch my arms across the ceramic. Although I'm experiencing a fabulous evening overall, this dynamic fills me with sadness, and I desire some seclusion. I pump the soap dispenser and lather. There's blood on these hands, and regardless of how vigorously I scrub, it'll never wash off. I snatch the towel from the rack and dry. Attempting to replace it, I meet my reflection and freeze.

Tomorrow marks the tenth anniversary of the deaths of my mother and father. Ten full years bereft of the people that raised me and placed me on a pedestal. My eyes swell again, scrutinizing the man in the mirror. Once upon a time, I thought I knew him. I now recognize I've been lying. And while you can run with a lie, you can't hide from the truth.

Sooner or later, the past catches up to you. When it does, what then? Completely righting my wrongs is impossible, yet I'm dedicating myself to remembering, just the same. I owe it to Gabriel. I owe it to my parents. Ultimately, I owe it to me. And with any luck, Darby walks alongside every step of the way.

It goes without saying there's nothing in life that's guaranteed, and nobody can predict the future. But if I'm certain of anything, it's come next December, I'll most definitely *not* be traveling back to Marfa, Texas… Or will I?

ABOUT THE AUTHOR

STEVEN MARKOFF

was raised in Toledo, Ohio and graduated from THE Ohio State University. He's an entertainment industry veteran who currently splits his time between Clarksdale, Mississippi, and Nashville, Tennessee. Markoff enjoys 80s Mickey Rourke films, sports, the music of Jeff Buckley, dogs, and not much else. *Marfa Lights* is his debut novel.